CREE

CREE

To Believe in the World

A NOVEL

VERENA ANDERMATT CONLEY

CREE
TO BELIEVE IN THE WORLD

iUniverse books may be ordered through booksellers or by contacting:

iUniverse
1663 Liberty Drive
Bloomington, IN 47403
www.iuniverse.com
1-800-Authors (1-800-288-4677)

ISBN: 978-1-4917-4838-1 (sc)
ISBN: 978-1-4917-4837-4 (hc)
ISBN: 978-1-4917-4836-7 (e)

Library of Congress Control Number: 2014917205

Printed in the United States of America.

iUniverse rev. date: 01/08/2015

What we most lack is a belief in the world, we've quite
lost the world, it's been taken from us.
—Gilles Deleuze

Contents

PART IV

PART V

Preamble

Dear Ami,

I met a man up north. His name was Cree. He profoundly changed my life. He helped me reconnect with myself and with the world. Just weeks ago, I left the city in solitude and despair. Now I have returned with a feeling of sadness but also with joy. One month ago, at a reception, I felt I had lost the world . . .

PART I

1

A Reception

E LLE LEANED BACK in the dark blue velvet wing chair and slowly scanned the living room of Elmwood, the residence of Rawling Moulter III, president of the prestigious Lincoln University. Along with the core of high-profile administrators, the room was spiked with academic stars, Nobel laureates, and recipients past and present of the MacArthur Fellowship, casually referred to as the "genius grant." The president had summoned them all to his mansion on this balmy evening in mid-August for a reception in honor of a delegation from the University of Beijing. The Chinese emissaries were visiting the campus to explore the possibility of a collaboration between the two universities.

For the occasion, Rawling Moulter III had invited those whom he proudly called his showcase faculty and administrators. He had gathered them in the vast living room of his colonial mansion, an architectural oddity in this part of the country, where the norm was Tudor and prairie styles inspired by Frank Lloyd Wright. The dark and stately room, furnished with a mixture of genuine antiques and reproductions, was designed to inspire awe. The wing chairs and Victorian sofas, in patterns of blue and rust, were matched by oversized oriental rugs that muffled people's steps and the sound of their voices. Several original paintings adorned the walls. Portraits of past presidents, clergymen, and donor couples, whose eyes scoured the room and seemed to keep the guests in check, were complemented with nineteenth-century American nature paintings and a few obligatory minor Impressionist landscapes. A dozen bouquets of white roses, expertly displayed on tables and dressers in large silver urns, lent the gathering an officially festive air. The hundred or so people assembled had dispersed into several small groups. Some were standing or sitting around the living room; others had congregated beyond the open French doors on the terrace, under beige market umbrellas from which garlands of tiny lights were hanging.

The thirteenth president of Lincoln University, Rawling Moulter III, was a tall, robust man with a receding hairline and piercing gray eyes. He wore stylish suits but always managed to look badly dressed. Recently widowed—his wife had died of cancer—he had a roaming eye. His attraction to Elle escaped no one. Elle knew that she owed her invitation to this exclusive reception in no small part to the privileged status she enjoyed with the president. A mere professor of sociology, Elle might not have been worthy of the A-list of invitees. Moulter's arrival on campus two years earlier had coincided with Elle's separation and divorce from her husband, Max, after nearly twenty years of marriage. Now that she was single, men had started to show renewed interest in her. She was aware of the president's elective affinity but had managed to keep him at a distance. Again, that day, she pretended not to notice his maneuvers. Her divorce had been finalized only a few months earlier, and she wanted to be left alone.

After Elle had made the rounds at the reception, she sat by herself, and from her wing chair, she noticed that the lamps on the end tables were already lit as the last rays of sunlight streamed into the room through the tall windows and the open French doors. She watched waiters clad in dark slacks and white shirts topped by black bow ties glide silently around the room. They were balancing trays with Champagne in crystal flutes and others laden with heavy hors d'oeuvres. Refusing the catered crab cakes that were offered her for the third time, Elle continued to take in the scene. She looked at the colleagues assembled.

The dean of humanities, a potbellied man with sandy combed-back hair and striped trousers that seemed on the verge of falling down, was arguing with the chair of political science about the role of sports on campus. The latter, cultivating an affected British accent, dismissed sports as nonacademic. Another faculty member, a winner of several book prizes that had enabled him to buy a summer house on a northern lake, smiled patiently at his female interlocutor, who was haranguing him about the merit of several architects and the construction of a contemporary arts center. Elle heard the shrill voice, pitched ever higher after the intake of several glasses of Champagne, of the wife of the dean of education. Turning her head slightly, she saw the stocky woman with her dyed blonde curls bobbing up and down as she tried to seduce the dean of the divinity school, who happily returned her advances. He too was obviously under the influence of the Napa Valley Champagne. He nudged the woman with his elbow and looked deep into her blurry blue eyes.

From a group of people standing near the large bay window at the far end of the room and who, judging from the intermittent laughter, seemed to be the only ones exchanging jokes, emerged a tall man in his late forties. Kirk Haywood was a named professor of psychology and trusted ally of the president. He had dark curls, an expensive tan, and a full smile that revealed two rows of perfect teeth. Kirk moved in higher circles. He sat on every foundation and was never denied a promotion or a grant. Glass in hand, he made his way over to Elle, who was absorbed as much in the spectacle as in her own thoughts.

Kirk liked Elle. A divorced man himself, he had let her know on several occasions that he would be interested in romance. Elle always declined politely. Kirk always accepted her rebuffs. Flashing his white teeth, he laughed each time in perfect measure with the cadence of the communication. "Still in mourning?" he'd say. "I'll wait. You will see—you'll change your mind."

Elle would protest, answering that she was disillusioned with the world and with men. To Kirk's new advances that evening, she replied with a faint smile. "You know," she reiterated, "I've given up on men."

"Oh, no, you haven't," Kirk answered. "For a woman like you, that is utterly impossible. Still going on that wilderness trip?" he added after a slight pause. Elle nodded. "Well, I hope you'll find happiness in the wilds. And don't let the mosquitoes bite you!" Kirk was alluding to Elle's upcoming trip to the Boundary Waters Canoe Area, a large wilderness in northern Minnesota, along the Canadian border. Laughing and shaking his curly head, he walked away. Before joining another group, he turned around one more time. Still grinning, he leaned forward and raised his finger, whispering in her direction, "Remember, I will always be here."

Elle knew the crowd assembled in the president's mansion well. She knew their professional achievements and their personal stories. Scanning the scene, she thought of all their successes and failures and who was cheating on whom. She remembered too well the pains and heartaches similar to her own, buried under the vanity of worldly glory. She had no desire, she said to herself, to join that crowd again, much less to embark on any relationship. The divorce had ravaged her. To forget, she had plunged even more into her work and dedicated herself to the education of her two teenage children: Josh, nineteen, and Amber, who had just turned eighteen.

A month ago, much to her own surprise and that of her colleagues, she had accepted an invitation from *Travel Magazine* to spend ten days in the Boundary Waters. Elle knew one of the editors of the magazine and had been asked to draft a substantial educational and promotional piece on the area. The wilderness was not exactly her area of expertise. As a sociologist, she dealt with urban environments, the knowledge of which she gleaned from spreadsheets and data. Yet Elle had the requisite writing skills to do the task. After some hesitation, she accepted. She would be part of a group of six writers, scientists, and photographers who, under the guidance of local experts, would visit the region and work together on the piece. Judging from the pictures she found on the web, the fabled area held promise of natural beauty, peace, and harmony. The clear, brilliant water of creeks, placid lakes, and red sunsets would provide a good escape and help her reconnect with herself.

She asked Josh and Amber if they wanted to come along. They all needed, she ventured, some family time before they dispersed in the coming academic year. To her surprise, both readily agreed. Josh asked to bring his girlfriend, Emily. Amber never even balked. Since her parents' divorce, Amber had developed a strangely protective attitude toward her mother. She would not let most people approach her mother, especially men. If one tried when she was around, she would circle around him like a watchdog and growl until the poor suitor abandoned his pursuit. Whether she sought to protect her newly found freedom away from paternal authority or whether she acted out of love for her mother—a feeling mixed perhaps with a tinge of rivalry—was unclear. In any case, she had become her mother's bodyguard. Watching Amber, Elle was alternately aggravated and amused. At times, she even found Amber's childish zeal endearing.

The sun was about to set behind the tall trees beyond the terrace of Elmwood. Its last rays cast an orange hue over the living room. The tiny lights under the three market umbrellas on the terrace began to glow brighter in the early evening hour. Feeling a sudden urge to leave, Elle decided to look for Rawling Moulter III. From across the room, she saw that he was still wooing the Chinese, who seemed impressed by his rhetoric. Remembering to smile right and left, she made her way across the large room to shake the president's plump hand.

"My dear Elle," Rawling Moulter III said, "you are ravishing as always. Must you leave already?"

Elle nodded and muttered the customary words of thanks for the wonderful reception. She bowed toward the Chinese while adding some words about hoping to see them in Beijing soon.

The president excused himself from his guests and personally escorted Elle to the door. He continued to squeeze her hand while they waited for a young attendant to fetch her white Jeep. Elle disengaged herself, jumped in her truck, and, waving one last time through the open window, sighed in relief as she aimed her vehicle down the gravel driveway and began the forty-five-minute drive home.

2

Driving Home

D RIVING DOWN THE quiet, deserted street lined with healthy elm trees and stately mansions, Elle glanced at the rows of Tudor and prairie-style houses set in deep and shady yards. The people living in these structures were clearly wealthy. But were they happy? How many dramas were being played out behind the thick brick-and-stucco walls, the fashionable awnings, and the beautifully landscaped yards? Tall impatiens in various shades of purple, lilac, orange, and white seemed to be the trend in flowers this year. They adorned nearly every entrance in large terra-cotta urns. She smiled. All these people tried so hard to be different, just to end up looking like everyone else on the block.

Elle left the residential area and turned onto a busy through street that led her to Lakeshore Drive and from there, along the edge of the water, to her apartment building located in the northern part of the city. Knowing the road well, she set her thoughts adrift for a moment.

She and her ex-husband, Max, had always disliked suburban living. Right after they were married, they bought an apartment on the tenth floor of a prewar brownstone in the Linden Park area on the now fashionable north side. They were city people, she liked to think, even before it became chic to be so. Max and Elle had married young. He was in his third and final year of law school at Lincoln. She had just graduated from Park University, twenty miles north, and was entering graduate school at Lincoln, where she wanted to specialize in urban studies. Their two children were born right away.

The first years were difficult, but Max soon made partner at Hoechst, Stanley, and Wick, a prestigious international law firm in the downtown area. With some extraordinary luck, Elle landed a position in her own department at Lincoln. Their careers took off, and for many years, colleagues jealously admired and criticized them for being the most handsome couple in their world. They had money, success, and two beautiful children. They seemed blessed with everything they ever wanted. The children were left in the care of a nanny—legal, Elle was quick to point out to friends and colleagues—while the parents devoted themselves to their careers and to all the socializing necessary to advance them. Max worked long hours and traveled extensively. In addition to teaching and writing, Elle ran an institute. They were everyone's ideal and envy—until one evening ...

There was a screeching sound of brakes. Someone honked excitedly. Elle awoke from her thoughts and sharply veered to the right. A gray Toyota passed her. The male driver inside was yelling and gesticulating wildly. Her heart still pounding from the near collision, Elle adjusted herself in her seat. She continued north on Lakeshore Drive and decided to pay more attention to the traffic, but she could not help herself from going over that fateful evening again ...

It had begun like a normal family night in mid-February, two years earlier. Josh had gone to a movie with his new friend Emily. Amber had retired early. She needed her sleep, she claimed, for her early-morning swimming practice. Amber swam backstroke for the Ramsey School and prided herself in her victories. She had earned so many ribbons that the walls of her room became a satin tapestry.

Elle and Max were working in their separate studies. Max was going over his dossier for a trial in Washington. He was to fly out early the following morning and had announced that he would be gone for several days. Sitting at her elegant Empire desk, Elle was reading the proofs of her new book on the status of what could be called "affordable housing" in midwestern cities. The greenish light that the glass shade of a banker's lamp cast on the desk gave her the impression of sitting in an intimate, protected zone.

It was the hour when calm was beginning to descend on the city. The traffic was still thick on Lakeshore Drive, ten stories below. Elle saw a stream of red taillights inching north and somewhat fewer headlights slowly making their way south. On the other side of the boulevard, she could make out the white-crested waves on the dark lake. Looking through the middle panel of the large glass window, Elle paused on her own reflection. Her thoughts strayed from the tedious task of proofing what she had written well over two years ago. She thought about her life, her career, her marriage, and her children. She came close to feeling happiness when she counted her worldly blessings. She had a handsome husband who made plenty of money. Josh and Amber were both A students at an exclusive private school—despite the fact that she was writing about urban plight and improving public education.

At forty-something, Elle had kept her good looks. She had a mass of wavy blonde hair and a good figure. The couple's relative wealth had enabled her to keep herself well groomed. She wore classy designer suits with seeming negligence. Yet she was also an advocate for social causes, something she had a little difficulty reconciling with a penchant for her fashionable demeanor. "Oh well," she chuckled as she brushed aside a strand of hair and a nagging doubt that seemed to stick to her skin. "One has to make a living." She continued reading her proofs.

Suddenly, the main telephone rang. Calls at this hour were rare. She decided to delay answering for a couple of rings. When she did pick up the receiver, she heard a woman's low voice say, "Darling, I can't wait until tomorrow."

"I know," came the laconic answer from a male voice that was clearly her husband's. A split second later, Max must have realized that someone—and that someone could only be Elle—was on the line. "Hmm," he said, clearing his throat. In a louder tone he added, "Yes, I will need that other dossier before I leave. Please bring it directly to the airport. I will see you tomorrow at seven thirty at the American Airlines counter. Thanks." There was a click, followed by silence.

Elle sat with the receiver in hand, dumbfounded. An operator's automated voice droned on: "If you would like to make a call, please hang up and dial again." Elle tried to shake off what seemed like a nightmare. Staring out over the dark lake, she became aware of the faint howl of the wind. The night now felt suddenly cold and forbidding.

She had to figure out what this was about. It might have been a misunderstanding. Resolutely, she pushed her desk chair back and with quick, decisive steps walked down to Max's office at the end of the hall. His door was open, as usual. He pretended to be focused on his files.

"Hi, hon!" Max sounded cheery.

Elle got straight to the point. Her voice quivered slightly when she asked the clichéd question she thought all women—except for her—had asked at least once in their lifetimes: "Who was *that* woman?"

"What woman?" Max grumbled without looking up.

"The one you were just talking to on the phone. She called you 'darling.'"

"You must be mistaken." Max looked up with the seductive boyish grin that she knew so well. Max also knew that it always made Elle melt. He used charm to try to reassure her. "It was my assistant, Evelyn. She called me on the house phone because my cell isn't working. She will drop off a brief at the airport tomorrow morning. It wasn't ready this afternoon when I left the office to come home and be with you."

"And why does she call you 'darling'?" Elle continued, wanting to believe Max but not feeling convinced.

"Did she? I didn't hear that." Max turned back to his work and seemed to ignore her presence.

"Max, are you lying? Are you seeing this woman? Is that why you've gone on so many business trips lately? Does this explain it all?" Elle suddenly felt like a jilted woman and, against her will, began to play the part. Her picture-perfect world was beginning to crumble. Her attempt at holding it together was in vain. Her knees gave in as she felt tears surge up in her. No, not now. Be strong ... To no avail. She was suddenly overcome with uncontrollable sobbing. "So that's what's happening. And I trusted you all this time. I trusted you. How could you ...?"

Abruptly, Max rose. A strand of his dark hair was hanging down over his high forehead; his lips were thin and his face drawn. He looked straight at Elle. "Yes," he said, almost brutally. "Yes, I am seeing Evelyn. She gives me support—emotional support." He paused as if to let the words sink in. When he resumed, the words began to gush forth. "You are always busy and never have time for me. All you do is think about yourself and your career. Evelyn admires me. She tells me she loves me. She needs me." In their twenty years together, Max had never spoken in these terms. Once he started, it seemed he could not stop. For the next ten minutes, as if someone had opened the floodgates, Max told Elle in an endless flow of words everything that he had seemingly held back for nearly two decades of marriage. Elle paid no attention to his needs. Evelyn was affectionate, she had time for him, and he reiterated that she was not always absorbed in her own stuff. And, yes, he was sick of this state of things.

Elle felt faint. However, she managed to compose herself, and she somewhat theatrically held out her arm, pointed her finger in the direction of the door, and ordered Max to get out. She heard herself speak and almost felt that she was playing on a stage. She really wanted him to come to her and to ask her for forgiveness. To her surprise, Max took her at her words.

"Very well, then. So it shall be," he answered. He looked around his study and picked up a few files and his briefcase. Ignoring Elle, he walked down the hall and entered their bedroom to fetch his suitcase, which was already packed for his trip. When he reemerged, he made his way straight toward the entrance door. Shaking the dark strand of hair out of his face, he put down his briefcase and luggage to open the door. Picking up his stuff, he gave her a quick glance over his shoulder and said somewhat ironically, "Good luck with your work." Then he exited.

Elle was aghast, unable to move. She heard more than she saw the door slam shut. The sound reverberated throughout her body. She knew her familiar world had ended. She was alone.

She decided to compose herself. Later she could give herself over to crying. She wanted to be careful not to wake Amber, who was sleeping. Josh would be home soon, and she did not want to let him see her like this. The children would ask questions. She would have to be evasive. Most of all, she needed time to regain self-control. She would answer her children's puzzled looks and inquisitive questions in the morning by saying that their father had left to catch an earlier plane. His absence the following day would be easy to explain. After that, she would have to be inventive …

As she turned onto Linden Terrace, the side street that led to her underground garage, Elle remembered the sleepless night she'd spent following Max's departure. She steered the car into her reserved slot, walked up a flight of stairs, and passed by the door attendant. "Hello, Pedro!" She tried to be charming.

"How is the senora"? He answered smilingly.

She took the slow elevator to the tenth floor and entered the apartment. The children had both gone out for the evening. Josh, back for the summer after his first year in college in New Hampshire, was out with Emily. They had found each other again after nearly nine months of separation. Amber, who had recently graduated from Ramsey, was staying over at a girlfriend's house. Elle put her purse down on the credenza near the entrance and kicked off her shoes. She walked down the hallway to her study and briefly looked toward the lake. It was quite dark by now, and the new moon barely shed any light on the calm waters. Elle paused on her reflection in the bay window.

3

Home Alone

THE APARTMENT WAS eerily quiet. Elle left the study and wandered down the long hallway, her steps muffled by the red oriental rug Max had brought back from Turkey after a successful litigation in Istanbul. She passed the empty living and dining rooms on the lakeside, casting a quick glance into the familiar kitchen. She and Max had spent many late nights sitting at the counter there, laughing together over a last drink after coming home from tedious social events or after long hours of labor. The kitchen now looked empty and unused. There was no smell of Max's cooking or his 4711 cologne. Elle poured herself a glass of wine and returned to her study.

The silence continued to overwhelm. The only sounds were those of the evening traffic from the boulevard ten stories below. It was a steady hum, punctuated by a cacophony of honking horns. Sitting in the semidarkness of the room, she studied her reflection. She thought of the lake and the beach where they had sat and played as a family while the children were growing up. Those had been happy days! They had perhaps not been exactly carefree; raising the children had been challenging. But the emotional support derived from having a family had buoyed her. She began to realize how much she had depended on Max's presence and on her family structure. Now Max was gone and the children were almost grown. Josh was already in college. In the fall, Amber would be a freshman at Berkeley. Elle would be alone. Suddenly, she dreaded the moment when the children would leave, the very moment that she and Max had anticipated jokingly as the moment of access to "their freedom." Her world had fallen apart just when she was about to reach the threshold of that freedom.

After his departure that night, Max never came back. He communicated by telephone that he wished to move out, and he asked for a divorce. He had found the woman of his dreams, and thus a return to Elle was impossible. Elle had a hard time explaining to the children that their dad was leaving. They all knew Evelyn, Max's assistant, and were disconsolate at the news—though Amber began to confide a few details. She recounted that when she and Josh had gone to the zoo with their dad years earlier, Evelyn had accompanied them. One day they had even gone to her apartment. She had looked at their dad longingly. They hadn't dared tell Elle because they felt she might be hurt. Elle reassured them that this was just a passing fancy. Their father would change his mind. She resisted the idea of a divorce. She was convinced that Max would reverse his decision and come back home. How could he help but do so? She was wrong.

The divorce dragged on for months. It turned quite messy. Elle began to see a side of Max she had never suspected. Over time, grief changed to anger. The man she had known for twenty years looked very different. He fought her hard in court and was merciless in his demands for a settlement. She had to struggle for her survival and even that of the children. At last, she was awarded the apartment, but Max vowed not to pay a cent for the children's college educations. Since Josh and Amber were siding with their mother, as he put it, he was exonerated from giving them any support. Elle failed to see the logic, but Max was determined.

Elle came out of her divorce with a bitter taste. She struggled with the blow to her ego and was only slowly adapting to single life with her children. She put up a good front and never let Josh and Amber see, or so she thought, how devastated she was. The children went through difficult times at first but then settled into their new routines. The frequent pizza dinners seemed to delight them even more than Max's gourmet dishes. This summer, however, Elle had truly noticed that Josh and Amber were turning into young adults. Soon the time would come when they would no longer be home for the summer. How would she adjust to their absence and to being completely alone?

It was to overcome a feeling of solitude and at times even despair, as well as to break out of the lonely and brooding existence she had led since Max's departure, that Elle accepted the assignment in the Boundary Waters. The trip promised to bring a change that would restore body and soul.

PART II

4

Northbound

A FEW DAYS AFTER the reception at the president's house, Elle was driving north in her Jeep, Amber in the front passenger seat. Josh and Emily were huddling together in the back. The baggage area was filled with blue, yellow, and red duffle bags, overstuffed L.L. Bean backpacks, and boxes of books, magazines, and games all piled so high that she could barely see through the rear window and had to maneuver with the side mirrors.

Amber was listening to music on her iPod while being mysteriously engrossed in a French novel that her teacher had given her for summer reading. It must be an old French teacher, Elle deduced from the title: *Bonjour Tristesse*. She remembered reading the same story in a class decades earlier. Written by Françoise Sagan, who was barely an adult at the time it was published, the story that scandalized Elle's parents' generation was about the coming of age of an adolescent girl on the French Riviera. The girl, whose mother had died, spends the summer with her father. She lives her first love story but at the same time becomes increasingly jealous of her father's new woman friend. She loves her father but dislikes the new woman giving her orders.

After meddling in her father's love affair, she succeeds in making the intruder leave.

Elle remembered vividly the Technicolor scenes from Otto Preminger's film version. Jean Seberg's short-cropped hair and striped T-shirts, Elle's mother had recalled, became everyone's fashion statement for several years. Elle recalled Deborah Kerr, the older woman, fleeing from the villa in her white convertible, driving over the cliffs and plunging into the Mediterranean. An accident? A suicide? The question was left open.

With the long dark hair that she had inherited from Max, Amber bore little resemblance to Jean Seberg, yet she had a penchant for drama and for manipulating people. She did not always seem to realize the effect she had on those around her. Elle had noticed in recent months how Amber bruised several young men who were beginning to pine after her. She looked sideways at her daughter. Even without physically resembling the young actress in the movie, Amber was often just as insouciant as the character in Françoise Sagan's story. She was also intransigent, at times even menacing. Most young men were clearly no match for her. Elle sighed. Her daughter had some growing up to do.

In the backseat, Josh and Emily were giggling and cooing. Unlike his sister, Josh was a quintessentially nice guy who seduced the world with his charm. Surreptitiously looking in the rearview mirror, Elle watched her son and his girlfriend. They were holding hands, alternately kissing lightly, and gazing deep into each other's eyes. *Young love*, Elle thought gloomily. She had been like that when she met Max. They must have looked almost like Josh and Emily, though at the time, she felt so grown up, so mature. Why did these two look so young to her? Elle sighed again while looking straight ahead at the wide flat highway that stretched seemingly endlessly toward the receding horizon.

They turned onto more winding secondary roads and entered tourist areas where lakes and forests alternated with small towns that advertised cabins, canoe rentals, fishing, and home cooking. The towns all had speed limits and even traffic lights, which made for slow driving. They passed through some fashionable areas advertised occasionally in the Sunday Travel sections of the *New York Times,* including one where Elle had spent a weekend with Max during their student years. They had rented inner tubes and floated down a popular river. They had pulled out of the water to escape the hot sun and had made love in the shade of a pine tree. With the memory, a sharp nagging pain returned.

When they crossed the bridge into Duluth, Elle urged the young people to take in the view of Lake Superior. This time, they deigned to raise their heads. "Wow," Josh exclaimed, "look at the silos and the tankers!" They stopped briefly on the waterfront and ordered handmade ice cream in a small coffee shop, a local rival of Starbucks, with its rough-hewn pine tables and benches advertising the forests of the area.

Back in the car, Amber grew impatient. "How much longer, Mom?" she inquired, now squirming in her seat. "This is boring."

Elle tried to be educational by informing them they were now entering the Iron Range. She told them about mining and courageous workers, especially women, and pointed out mountains of slag heaps. She was ignored when she mentioned Bob Dylan.

Amber, who had given up on her book, was completely enraptured in her music. She was gesticulating and bobbing up and down to rhythms unknown to Elle's generation, which were streaming from her iPod into her ears. Josh and Emily were sleeping peacefully on each other's shoulders. The Jeep sped north effortlessly on yet another wide highway, this one lined by spruce and aspen trees. The soothing, rhythmic clicking sound the car produced as it rolled over the joints of the asphalt plates put even Amber to sleep. With no one to talk to, Elle checked out the local radio stations. Local broadcasts talked about fishing, mining, and problems of the logging industry. She listened for a while, sympathetic to the plight of the region, before turning the radio off and giving herself over to her thoughts again.

In spite of her professional achievements, Elle had led a sheltered life. After Max's abrupt departure, the void she felt grew deeper and wider. Though she had opportunities to go out, with the exception of official functions like the president's reception, Elle kept mainly to herself. She had lost weight and looked pale. Kirk Haywood had told her that her new "longing look" was intriguing. She had smiled wearily. Had the breakup made her wiser? She deliberately remained celibate and convinced herself that she enjoyed her new status. Even though the comforting benefits of a relationship had also vanished, it demanded less effort. Yet had her marriage with Max been that comforting? Had he really given her the emotional support she thought she remembered? She began to rethink their years together. Max was the A type with whom sparks were always flying. Based on raw success and narcissistic glory, the world they had built for themselves now seemed shallow.

Elle sighed again and snapped out of her reverie. Everyone was still dozing around her. She took another sip from the silver Starbucks coffee mug in the cubbyhole behind the gearshift to keep herself awake. After driving through more small towns organized around gas stations displaying plenty of "beer and bait" signs, she finally reached a settlement heralding itself with an oversized sculpture of a sunfish. Her instructions told her to turn onto a county road that wound around several small lakes shining bright blue in the afternoon sun. *This really is the land of sky-blue waters*, Elle thought, recalling the old advertisement for Hamm's beer. Near a bar that announced itself as the Sportsman's

Last Chance, she turned onto the Echo Trail, an unpaved road that was one of the two wilderness trails in northern Minnesota, just south of the Canadian border.

The vibrations from the grooves left by road graters woke everyone up. "Are we *theeeere* yet?" This was the common question, inflected with growing impatience. Elle reassured them and urged them to look at the glistening streams and marshes bordered by dark ridges of black spruce and tamarack. A few glances in their direction drew more yawns from her passengers.

At last, they reached the top of a small hill with a sign for Loon Lodge. Before turning onto a dirt road that would finally lead them to their destination, Elle pointed out a tall tree spreading its massive branches on the far side of the county road. "See, guys, this must be a first-growth tree. It's a white pine and is probably over two hundred years old. Minnesota used to be covered with these trees." She proudly shared the information she had downloaded from the web when she checked out the Boundary Waters to decide whether to accept the offer from *Travel Magazine*.

"Get off it, Mom," responded Amber laconically, while Josh, forever seductive, expressed admiration over his mother's tree lesson.

"You can dead-end right into it if you come down the road from the lodge. Dead man's tree! Ha-ha!"

They finally arrived at the iron swing gate to Loon Lodge. After slowly maneuvering the car down a dusty and winding path and through a stand of tall Norway pines and rounding yet another bend, she found herself suddenly in a gravel area adjacent to the lodge. It was as if she had been transported into a fairy-tale world. "Wow," she could not refrain from whispering.

"Wow," the youngsters echoed. The beauty of the place was clearly lost on no one.

They checked out the large log cabin–style lodge next to a pond on which white ducks were swimming. A small wind turbine was turning on top of a pole sunk into the ground in a patch of neatly trimmed grass. Here, deep in the woods, wind generated electricity. The glow of strategically planted wildflowers illuminated the scene. Having finally overcome an unforeseen sense of wonder, Elle parked in front of the main entrance. They all scrambled out of the car and busied themselves with the cargo.

5

Loon Lodge

A PORTLY MAN in his mid- to late forties, with blondish hair, baby blue eyes, and a shiny round face, opened the main door of the lodge. He descended three or four wooden steps and, smiling good-naturedly, extended his hand to introduce himself. "Hi, I'm Tom Silver. I'm the owner of Loon Lodge. You must be Elle Baxter."

"Yes." Elle smiled and shook his hand. "And these are my children, Josh and Amber. And this is their friend Emily," she added.

"Welcome to Loon Lodge," said Silver. "My wife, Jenny, and I will do all we can to make your stay comfortable." He called in the direction of the lodge: "Jenny, come on out—the Baxters are here!" He turned toward Elle and the children again. "Jenny and I are so pleased to have you here. You can park your car over there under the pine trees." He gestured to an area in the back of the house. "I'll help you with your bags and show you to your cabins."

Elle parked the car in the designated area and returned to meet Jenny, a rotund red-haired woman in her late thirties, who was already making friends with Josh, Amber, and Emily by asking them what their favorite dishes were.

"Okay, folks," Tom interrupted, laughing. "Let's go down to the cabins and get you settled." He grabbed a few of the heavier pieces of luggage and started on the path in the direction of the cabins.

"I'll go and finish supper," Jenny said. "See ya," she added with a genuine "Minnesohtan" inflection that Elle recalled from Garrison Keillor's *Prairie Home Companion*.

As they passed the corner of the lodge, the appetizing aroma of home cooking diffused from one of the windows. Amber sighed in anticipation. "It seems as if we've arrived in paradise," she joked wryly. They filed down a narrow path along a rocky hillside covered with tall and slender red pine trees, punctuated with birch, aspen, and rarer maple trees, beyond which the waters of a lake glistened in the early evening sun.

Loon Lodge was built on a bluff overlooking a good-sized lake. In addition to the lodge, a handful of small cottages dotted its western shores. The rest, Tom informed them, was wilderness. The eight guest cabins were situated on a slope slightly below the main building and spaced about the woods. Privacy was guaranteed. The youngsters would occupy a small two-bedroom cabin, and Elle would have a one-bedroom cabin to herself. Their cabins were both at the western end of the property, a short distance from each other and a couple of hundred yards from the main lodge. The other cabins were located on the eastern side. In addition to its exquisite natural setting, Loon Lodge prided itself on its immaculate cabins and savory cuisine. Her body aching and her mind spent, Elle now looked forward to the "tender loving care" promised in the pamphlet that had been sent her as part of the information about the trip.

They first stopped at Black Bear, the cabin where Josh, Amber, and Emily would be staying. Tom proudly opened the door and signaled for them to enter. They all dutifully lavished praise on what they saw. In the sitting room, sparkling windows through which blue waters shined were complemented by spotless wooden floors. A stone fireplace lent the interior a cozy air. An old-fashioned Victorian-style sofa with a reddish velvet cover added a touch of elegance.

"North Wood chic!" exclaimed Amber with a laugh. Josh and Emily voiced their delight. Elle smiled and left them all to their unpacking. She felt she had made the right decision in coming here.

Tom Silver escorted Elle to her own cabin, the fabled Whispering Pines. As he unlocked the door, a loon cried in the distance. Elle shuddered from both pleasure and an unknown fear. "How do you like it?" Tom Silver asked in his direct manner, his voice suddenly sounding distant.

"It's simply wonderful," Elle answered belatedly and somewhat absentmindedly. Since the divorce, she had tried to hide her anguish underneath a smile.

"We try to make our guests happy," the proud owner confessed. "You have time to freshen up. Dinner is served at seven o'clock in the main lodge. Drinks are at six thirty on the deck. You'll meet the other guests as well. Your entire party is already here. See ya!" He waved his hand and pulled the door shut behind him.

Elle took her bags to the cozy bedroom, furnished with a rustic double bed covered with an olive, beige, and brown quilt, where she would sleep by herself. She quickly retreated to the main sitting room and looked around. A blue oversized armchair with a reading lamp looked inviting. Another Victorian sofa, this one covered in red with a paisley motif, faced a stone fireplace. Above it, the sight of two crossed snowshoes brought a smile. Through a large paneled window, between the pine trees, she glimpsed the sheen of the lake. She decided that the desk positioned against the wall near the entrance door would be her workstation. Elle had read that there were no telephones in the cabins.

The cell phone, it turned out, was also out of range. The lodge was situated in a small pocket on the map where wireless phones were not working. Next year, Tom Silver had assured his guests apologetically, the problem would be remedied.

"Not to worry," Elle had said, brushing off Tom's display of guilt. She would make her calls in the main lodge, where there was a small office station reserved for the guests. She figured that it would even be fun for a few days. She could take a break from her electronic gadgets. In any event, she only expected a call from her mother, who was about to go visit Elle's sister, Ami, in San Francisco.

After a long day of driving, Elle sank into the armchair that seemed to welcome her tired body. The light of the late afternoon sun illuminated the entire room. Overwhelmed, she convinced herself that the serenity would help heal her bruised soul. Nature would calm her overwrought nerves. She would reconnect with her children and with herself. At the same time, the children would have a week of hiking, canoeing, kayaking, and swimming that would replenish their energies for the long winter to come. It would benefit everyone.

She reluctantly rose to splash cold water on her face and smooth her hair back. It was time to go meet the other guests.

6

Meeting the Guests

ELLE ASCENDED THE narrow path to the main lodge. Near the top of the hill, the path divided. The upper fork led to the main entrance of the building and the parking lot, the lower one to a set of stairs in front of the lodge that gave access to a large open deck overlooking the lake. Elle followed the lower fork and climbed up to the deck, where rustic chairs and small tables were elegantly displayed. Around one of the larger tables, sipping beer and wine, several of the guests were already gathered. Tom Silver had informed Elle that of the remaining six cabins, the other participants of the *Travel Magazine* project occupied three. The last three were rented to other guests.

Elle tried to decipher the scene. The group assembled on the deck looked as if they might be her new colleagues. A tall, burly man, a glass of white wine in hand, rose to greet Elle. "Hello," he said jovially. "I'm Mike Turnbull. You must be Elle Baxter. Well, well. We've been waiting for you. Come and meet the rest of the Boundary Waters gang. Hey, guys, here she is at last. I'd say that she was well worth waiting for," he added with a laugh, steering Elle with his free hand in the direction of the group. "She is even more beautiful than we thought she would be." He winked. "With a name like that, how can it be otherwise?"

Used to hearing comments with innuendos, Elle answered with a weary smile and thanked him. She approached the table around which, it turned out, the entire group of the Boundary Waters Project had gathered.

These people would be her companions for the next ten days. They would work on a common project and even go on a three-day trip together. They all seemed to come in couples. Mike Turnbull, who'd made the introductions, was from Milwaukee, where he worked as a freelance journalist. He and Elle would be the designated writers.

He gestured around the table to introduce Linda, his plumpish girlfriend with short-cropped blonde hair and Levi cutoffs, who clearly took an immediate and irreversible dislike to Elle. While sensing her animosity, Elle acknowledged her presence with a courteous smile.

There were the photographers for the project, Rod Sharp and Brett Love, his companion, both from New York. The pair had been on nature trips together before and decided to commit to the project out of a genuine desire to explore this wilderness. Rod and Brett were the typical East Coast nature photographers. Tall, thin with impeccably cut wavy hair combed back, they wore the appropriate stylish gear and displayed slightly affected manners but were good sports when it came to socializing with the group.

Jim Cleaver, a blue-eyed man sporting a thick graying beard, and Joan Bennett, a middle-aged woman with a trim, wiry body, short sandy hair, and large almond-shaped eyes, were the environmental scientists from San Francisco. They would add the scientific data to Mike and Elle's account and to the photographs. Jim was married, but as Elle would learn later from Mike, he had been having an affair with Joan for years. The two liked to go on assignments to spend time together, unbeknownst to Jim's spouse, who refused to grant him a divorce.

"I say, this is nature at its best, isn't it?" declared Mike, who was the life of the party. "So, Elle, we've introduced ourselves. Your turn! What's your story? What made you want to be part of this expedition?"

"I just wanted to get away from the city, I suppose."

"Oh, summer in the city! Was it a little hot down there?" ventured Mike. A quick outburst of laughter followed, ending in a moment of silence. "Want some wine?" Mike offered. Elle acquiesced, and Mike promptly poured her a glass. "Oh, I guess it's a little too full," he chuckled, looking at the glass, which was now filled nearly to the brim. "Not quite how they teach you in those tasting classes, right? So are you here alone?"

"No, I'm with my two children and one of their friends," Elle replied, her eyes searching for the youngsters, who were nowhere in sight.

"Well, isn't this nature at its best!" Mike repeated in an obvious attempt to fill the silence. "Happy hour with a sunset." Another chorus of laughter followed. "Care for another glass of delicious … what is it?" He held up the bottle to read the label: "Crane Lake Chardonnay, Napa Valley. Oh, whatever. It's alcohol." Elle could not repress a smile. "Pull up a chair," Mike invited with a gesture of his hand.

She grasped a free chair and sat down among this happy group. Again, from afar, the cry of a loon punctuated the air. Elle shuddered for the second time. *A perfect cliché*, she thought, but how mysterious and haunting that call was. It really gripped one's insides.

"Where are your children?" Joan asked in her husky voice.

"Oh, they're around," Elle rejoined, gesturing toward their cabin and the lake.

"So you're a teacher," said Mike. "Lots of free time, hmm? Is that why you're here? Looking for something to do?"

Knowing better than to enter into this kind of provocation, Elle demurely looked around the table at the group of people that chance had brought together.

The wind picked up and swept through the pine trees. *They actually do whisper,* Elle noted with an inward smile. *It's not just a fallacy.*

"Hey, Elle," she heard Mike challenge her, "tell us a little more about yourself. What's a good-looking lady like you doing here alone?"

She cringed, but just at that moment, she heard her children call from the path below. They had already tested the water and emerged from the lake clean and sparkling. *They make a handsome trio,* Elle thought proudly as she watched them climb the path. Amber was ahead of the other two. Her long dark mass of hair was hanging down her back. She moved up the hill in big strides. There was something both passionate and pugnacious about her. *How will she ever do in love,* Elle wondered with a sigh.

Josh and sweet Emily, as they had dubbed her, followed a few steps behind. During his first year in college, Josh had turned into a tall, handsome young man with a full head of wavy sandy-brown hair and sparkling brown eyes. He and Emily, with her angel face, blue eyes, and long blonde ringlets, were inseparable. They had met two years earlier at a party. It was their first love, a love at first sight that had weathered their first separation.

She introduced them to the others as they joined them. It did not escape Elle that Amber checked out the scene, surveying any potential danger, especially from Mike. After introductions were made, the trio sat down at a table at the far end of the deck and resumed an animated conversation about the respective merit of two hip-hop groups. A young man who looked at the world through thick horn-rimmed glasses came up the stairs and asked to join them. He was accepted into the group. Elle overheard him introduce himself as Lyle Amman. He lived in

Cincinnati, but his mother was from this area, so they had come here for a brief family vacation. He was eager to let them know he had just finished his first year at Oberlin College and was afraid he would be terribly bored in the woods. He seemed happy to have their company.

Elle felt her body relax. The effect of the Chardonnay spread slowly through her limbs. The calm of the setting was soothing. She silently congratulated herself again for having come here.

From the kitchen side of the lodge, the sound of a bronze bell, loud enough to be heard from any part of Loon Lodge, interrupted the flow of conversations. The chime brought the remaining guests back from the lake and out of their cabins. Quick introductions were made soon after that. Elle and the youngsters met the other three families: Lyle's parents, Otto and May Amman, and his two younger siblings, Ashley and Chris. Randy and Sarah Daniels, from Madison, Wisconsin, were there with their young twin girls, Rachel and Zoe. A thirty-something couple, Mark Spitzer and Sophie Grozier, were visiting from Iowa City. They all nodded and grinned before filing into the dining hall through the open sliding doors.

The aroma bore promise. They sat down with high expectations at four large wooden tables. Jenny, as the main cook, was assisted by Marge, Betsy, and Ruth, her trusted local helpers, who began by serving a creamy vegetable soup. The group fell quiet in the dining hall for a couple of minutes, but it wasn't long before the chatter of voices resumed.

Elle listened. She overheard snatches of conversation from others about pollution and crime in the city, about sending one's children to the ideal college, and the splendor of the wilderness. It felt good to be eating in a group of people again. When Marge, Betsy, and Ruth brought in the main course, the guests lavished praise for the chicken and wild rice casserole.

A beaming Jenny, wearing a long white apron over her jeans, emerged from the kitchen. "Just wait until tomorrow, folks," she grinned, affecting modesty.

The casserole made the conversation turn to the topic of ricing. Elle had never seen rice beds. There were some right here on the other side of the lake and even more in the rivers of the area, Tom informed her. Mike volunteered to take Elle by canoe to the rice beds across the lake anytime. Though he was not making passes at Elle, he clearly was aware of what he rightly assumed to be her single status. Mike's girlfriend, Linda, cringed. The tension eased when Marge, Betsy, and Ruth brought in several blueberry pies that would round out the guest's first culinary evening delight at the lodge. The women took special trouble to inform everyone that the berries had been handpicked.

Relaxed by the warmth of the food, wine, and the conversation, the guests stepped back out on the deck. The Ammans and the Danielses soon departed with their broods in the direction of their cabins. Mark Spitzer and Sophie Grozier, who were in an intense phase of courtship, left for the dock to admire the evening colors from a pair of strategically positioned Adirondack chairs. Elle and her group decided to stay out on the deck. Josh and Emily disappeared, but Amber stayed on. Lyle Amman decided to keep her company. He was visibly taken with Amber, who pretended to ignore him. They all sat around in their wooden deck chairs, facing west, where the last glimmer of light from the setting sun gradually faded.

The evening sky was soon riddled with stars and some brighter planets. They spotted the hazy white band of the Milky Way and some fast-moving satellites; they glimpsed the streak of light in the path of a shooting star.

"Make a wish!" exclaimed Joan, a scientist who clearly did not mind a little superstition. Elle could not resist.

"What did you wish for?" Mike asked her.

"Don't tell him," Joan interjected.

"Top secret," Elle replied flirtatiously.

"You didn't ask me," Linda protested sharply.

"Oh, don't take it that way," Mike grumbled, turning to Linda.

The conversation drifted until they gradually fell silent. They listened to the breeze in the trees, the lapping of the small waves, and the occasional cry of loons on the dark lake. The lone loon of the afternoon must have been joined by another, perhaps its mate.

Joan rose. "Tomorrow will be a long day," she reminded her new colleagues, who decided to follow her example.

Mike gave Elle a kiss on the cheek and a last look, and his voice gave a special inflection to the "good night."

Back in her cabin, Elle turned off the lights and listened to the wind in the trees. Slurping noises seemed to come from the water. Something scurried by her cabin. The call of an owl sounded in the distance. It was haunting and seemed to carry a sinister foreboding. She approached the window. She looked one more time at the infinite stars and the Milky Way in the moonless sky before she finally went to bed and lay awake for a long time, mulling over the last twenty years of her life.

7

The First Day

I N HER CITY life, Elle had the habit of starting the day with lap swimming at a nearby gym. Not wanting to break the routine, she decided to try the lake and ventured down the steep and narrow trail covered with a thick layer of pine needles that led from her cabin to a sandy beach. A solitary duck, sitting on a wooden dock, protested her arrival and fluttered into the water. Elle threw her beach towel on a weathered picnic table nearby and walked to the edge of the reddish, almost bloody-looking, lake. It was the iron ore, she remembered from her preliminary readings about the region, that lent the lakes and streams of this region their reddish tinge.

She put a foot in the water and watched tiny fish scurry in all directions. This was certainly different from the controlled environment of the chlorinated city pool. Bravely, Elle walked in to her waist. After some hesitation, she braced herself and dove into the cool waters. She pushed back up to the surface, blew a few bubbles, and exhaled. She swam out a few hundred yards and looked around. Bordered by distant pine-covered hills, the calm, serene lake stretched all around her.

She breathed again deeply, took a few more strokes, and returned
to land just as the sun was rising over the trees behind the lodge. It cast
its oblique rays through the top of the tallest trees and then gradually
began to illuminate the slope and the lake. On the shore, she shook off
the beads of water and wrapped herself in her towel.

Mike's baritone voice startled her. "Howdy, Elle! How's that water?"
He sized her up and down. "You're an early riser." Perhaps sensing that
Elle felt violated in her space, he added equivocally, "Well, I guess I'd
better be on my way." With a waving gesture, he turned and disappeared
in the direction of his cabin at the opposite end of the camp.

Elle was troubled by the sudden encounter. Mike's attention
was giving her a sense of pleasure that she refused to recognize. She
continued to breathe deeply as she walked back up to her cabin. The
clean air was beginning to replenish her aching city lungs with oxygen
and life. She carefully chose her outfit, a pair of faded boot-cut jeans,
a white T-shirt, and her Nikes. Prophylactically, she put on a fresh
swimsuit. After combing back her hair and brushing her teeth, she set
out for breakfast at the lodge.

Waiting for the guests, Marge, Betsy, and Ruth were putting last-
minute touches on the buffet, where Mike, who had been first to arrive,
was already loading his plate. When Elle entered, the women greeted
her cheerfully with their unmistakable accents. "Heya, Elle! Gone
swimming?"

"Yeah, the lady is quite athletic," Mike said, turning in her direction.
"In fact, how was that swim?" He snickered. "You looked pretty good."

Elle pretended not to hear their suggestive tone as she made her
way down the long side table that was full of fresh juices, blueberries,
and home-cooked cereal in addition to the standard fare of eggs with
bacon and home fries. "This stay is going to cleanse body and soul,"
Elle commented.

"Yeah, must be different from the city," Marge mused, shaking her head. "Don't know how you folks can stand it. All that crime."

Elle laughed as she inserted a slice of homemade bread in the toaster. She grabbed a mug that bore the inscription "Loon Lodge" in red letters set against the green outline of three spruce trees and filled it with coffee from the large urn. The brew was quite a contrast from the Starbucks that jump-starts city dwellers on the daily run to work. One could go on drinking the famous old-fashioned northern brew all day without getting the jitters or a racing heart. Elle sat down at one of the wooden tables on which several bouquets of black-eyed Susans with their bright yellow petals and dark brown centers were displayed in small cobalt-blue vases.

"Do you mind?" Elle heard Mike ask. She gestured.

Sitting next to her, he rearranged the toasted bread on his full plate and started digging into his eggs. Still chewing, he said, "Tom says we'll have two speakers for our first seminar, a regional specialist from the Department of Natural Resources and a teacher from a local college. They'll introduce us to the history, geography, and geology of the place. Tomorrow our guide will join us. Some local guy. Nice, I hear, and according to Tom, he's quite striking!" He turned to her and laughed.

Elle felt the undercurrent of his laughter. Her feelings about Mike were conflicted. Somehow, she was flattered by his attention. Yet, she persuaded herself, she needed calm to recover. She further reminded herself that Linda did not seem to appreciate Mike's interest in her, nor did Amber. How was she to proceed?

8

The Nature Seminar

L EAVING THE QUESTION open, Elle lingered over breakfast. She took several refills from the coffee urn while the other guests trickled in. Amber and even Josh and Emily arrived, still yawning and stretching. The Amman family took over its own table. The guests exchanged the usual niceties and extolled the quiet during the night. Lyle asked to sit next to Amber, who begrudgingly pushed her chair to the side. From behind his glasses, he could not take his eyes off the young woman who persisted in ignoring him. The youngsters' game had plainly not escaped Mike, who winked at Elle as a sign of complicity— but what complicity?

Back at her cabin, waiting for the first seminar to begin, Elle looked at the empty bedroom and paused at the sight of the unmade bed. She shrugged off a sudden fantasy and exited precipitously. On the way to the lodge, she stopped at Black Bear.

"Hey, Mom, what's up?" Amber's youthful voice rang out. "Josh, Emily, and I are going canoeing on the lake. Even boring Lyle said he would join us."

"Be careful," Elle replied.

"Of what?" queried Amber. "You know I'm a top swimmer, always first in my heat. As for the other stuff, you better watch out yourself," she added abruptly, even enigmatically, before returning to her sunscreen.

The three were excited about the day ahead. Josh spoke of taking a fishing rod, which made sweet Emily cringe. "The poor fish! You know I'm a vegetarian. How can you do this to me?"

Josh displayed his preppy laugh and comforted her. "For you," he said seductively, "I would do anything."

Their cabin had already been transformed into a young adults' lair. Clothes and her French book were strewn about Amber's room. In Josh and Emily's, a collection of magazines was neatly stacked in a corner. Elle left them while they were still laughing. Again she saw her children in a different light. They suddenly looked so grown up now that they were beginning to have their own amorous relations. Soon they would be gone. She sighed and pushed the thought out of her mind.

When she arrived at the lodge, the Ammans, minus Lyle, were getting ready for their outing. Dad was struggling to tie down a reluctant canoe on top of their Toyota minivan, while the two remaining children were climbing into the backseats, earbuds securely plugged into their ears. May Amman waved from the passenger side.

"See you tonight!" Elle shouted, waving back as she ascended the steps to the main entrance.

Tom Silver left the desk to direct her to the seminar room at the end of the hallway, past the souvenir rack and the telephone booth. Elle made her way to the sunny room furnished with a large knotted pine table surrounded by eight sturdy wooden chairs. Sipping coffee from Loon Lodge mugs, Joan and Jim were already seated on a bench covered by cushions with elk and bear motifs.

At the end of the table, the representative from the Department of Natural Resources was fumbling with his computer in preparation for the upcoming PowerPoint presentation. He turned to Elle with a grin and stretched out his hand. "You must be the one who's going to help write the story. I'm Tony Richardson, from the DNR. Pleased to meet you. We'll give you plenty of things to write about. This is Sherry, my assistant." He gestured toward a grinning stocky young woman whose ruddy complexion lent her a tough look in her drab olive uniform. In the meantime, Mike, Rod, and Brett had joined them. The last person to arrive was John Makala, a bearded, bespectacled teacher from the local junior college. After completing introductions with handshakes and waving gestures, they were ready to begin their first session.

John Makala pinned a large map on the board. The morning would be dedicated to the history of the region. John and Tony took turns telling the group about the wars between the Ojibway and the Sioux. They discussed how the French came to the region in the early eighteenth century to trade guns and trinkets for beaver pelts—traveling down from Montreal on the Saint Lawrence River, across the Great Lakes, and along the chain of Border Lakes, all the way to International Falls and, at times, to points farther west and south. Settlers arrived only at the beginning of the twentieth century.

Tony pointed to specific places on the large map while John held forth with the help of many PowerPoint illustrations. They featured old photographs of Eastern European immigrant families whose members were alternately grinning or looking stern, sitting in horse-led carriages and later in open Model T Fords, or standing next to their quarries of dead game. The two men discussed the successive waves of farmers, fishermen, and lumberjacks who populated the area. They spoke of the first environmentalists, whose dreams led to the creation of the Superior National Forest and, in 1973, to that of the Boundary Waters proper, followed in 1975 by the adjacent Voyageurs National

Park that comprised the larger Border Lakes separating the United States from Canada.

The group listened avidly to the presenters' lively narrative and delighted in their quaint and colorful pictures. They touched on myriad topics, from logging to tourism as well as the fate of a nearby Ojibway reservation. Elle took copious notes about local customs, blueberry picking, ricing, hunting, and smoking fish. When they broke for lunch, Tony informed them that the afternoon session would be devoted to geology.

Eager to take a quick stroll in the woods on her way to the dining hall, Elle left the lodge through the back entrance and crossed the grassy area dotted by a small pond on which half a dozen domesticated white ducks were happily swimming in front of red geraniums. It was like a picture from *Architectural Digest*! She followed a solitary path, and the sound of footsteps immediately startled her. She turned and saw the outline of a male figure. Her heart began to race madly before she recognized that it was Mike.

"Hey there!" he called out. "Wait for me. Need someone to walk with? I'll protect you from the bears." His broad grin was contagious. Elle laughed.

"What's this playing the loner? A beautiful lady like you? So what really brought you up here?" Mike inquired, seeming to sense that something was remiss. "No husband? Widowed?"

"Divorced," Elle answered curtly.

"Well, that puts us in the same boat, so to speak. Ha-ha. Around here, that can be taken literally," he added, laughing at his own joke and nodding his balding reddish-blond head. "Anyway, I just couldn't put up with the complaining anymore. Constant nagging. Had to leave. The kids never forgave me. It happened over two years ago, but they still won't talk to me." A cloud swept over Mike's face, and his broad grin vanished for a while.

By then, they had reached the lodge again. Voices, laughter, and the clatter of dishes and forks came from the dining hall. Leaning against the railing of the deck, Amber cast disapproving glances in the direction of her mother. Lyle, who had forfeited the family outing, stood at Amber's side, vainly trying to get her attention.

"And where did *you* go?" Amber asked her mother curtly.

"Oh, I just stretched my legs a bit after the seminar."

"In the *woods*," Amber commented wryly.

Mike appeared unperturbed. He waved and walked straight past the dark-haired fury and into the dining hall.

Elle patted her daughter on the shoulder. "Where are Josh and Emily?"

"They went canoeing. They won't be back until dinnertime. Lyle wanted me to go too, but I changed my mind."

"I see," Elle replied.

Young love, she thought again, not without a pang of jealousy. She bit her lip and sighed. Josh and Emily were already a little married couple. Amber was more difficult, like a volcano, always ready to erupt. Was she going to have her first romance this summer with Lyle? Was Lyle up to the part? Poor Lyle. He looked so serious behind his glasses and was just a little too eager to put up with Amber's whims.

Shadowed by Amber, Elle made her way to the lunch buffet. The colorful sight and appetizing aroma of an assortment of cheeses and salads artfully arranged on the table gave her a buoyant feeling. She took great care in constructing a salad, and with a glass of springwater in hand, she sat down with her new colleagues. Tony Richardson claimed the empty chair next to her and bit into his triple-decker sandwich.

"So how do you like it so far?" he asked between bites. "I bet it's better than the city, right? You have other things, I know, but not this." He made a wide circle with his hands. "Yep, this is a great spot. I'm glad you're going to write a story on our place." His blue eyes that looked deeply into hers were a trifle unsettling.

Just leave me alone, she pleaded silently. As if from a distance, she heard her own voice say, "Oh, yes, it will be great to be outdoors, to get to know a new area, and to be with this group and my children."

"Did your husband stay home to work?" Tony pried further. Elle made a face.

"The lady is here to forget," interjected Mike, who had been eavesdropping on the conversation.

"Oh, I see," he said. "So sorry." Realizing his blunder, Tony became very loquacious. He heaped a litany of praise on the beauty of the lakes with no human habitation, the purity of the landscape in the dead of winter, snowmobiling, and cross-country skiing.

Elle smiled patiently while Tony's voice droned on. She listened to the sounds around her while basking in the balmy air redolent with the scent of fresh pine. A gentle breeze was blowing. Her inner chatter began to subside. She glanced at Amber seated at the next table with Lyle. Sipping lemonade through a straw, Amber looked seductive with her tall well-shaped body, high cheekbones, and full lips. Lyle was trying to impress her with talk about his work on the college newspaper. His bragging was lost on Amber, whose disinterested air made him redouble his efforts. Elle heard Mike's voice as if from a distance. It was time to resume their seminar.

In the afternoon, Tony and John Makala told the group about the Unique bedrock geology that formed millions of years ago. They showed pictures of volcanic rock and granite formed from magma within the earth. These rocks, John insisted, could tell the story of great upheavals that finally led to the towering forests, abundant wildlife, and the presence of humans. They would explore this area during their day hikes and their longer trip. One of the best local guides, Tony reassured them, a young man who often led groups into the wilderness, would accompany them. He would join them the following morning and talk to them more about the place, especially its fauna and flora.

At the end of the session, Elle headed for the dock, where Josh and Emily were just pulling in. Having beached their canoe, they stood in the sand, kissing and holding each other tightly. *Young love—how wonderful,* Elle silently rehearsed the same refrain. Without the slightest embarrassment, Josh and Emily waved hello to Elle.

"Going for a swim, Mom? Come on." Josh rushed into the lake, followed by a screeching and laughing Emily. Their voices echoed eerily across the water. Soon the two were busy splashing and dunking each other. What youthful ardor. How did she even once possess it? How had it been lost? She took off her jeans and T-shirt and slowly waded into the cool lake. The soothing waters embraced her body for the second time that day. She swam out to where the two kids were playing their dunking game.

"Join us, Mom!" Josh shouted.

Laughing, Elle took off in the other direction. She put her head in the soothing current and floated for a while, looking up into a sky that was turning red at the horizon.

The children had long headed for their cabin when Elle reached the shore. It was Mike who greeted her.

"Hi there," he said in his jolly manner. "Gone for another swim?" Elle managed a smile. "I should have joined you," he grumbled. "It sure looks inviting." She nodded and wrapped her bath towel a little tighter. Almost as a non sequitur, he added, "Let's go canoeing tomorrow evening. I'll take you across the lake at sunset and show you the rice beds."

"All right, let's have a romantic outing," Elle heard herself say, somewhat to her own surprise. Shaking her hair back, she walked past Mike and followed the steep, narrow path to Whispering Pines. She remembered later that she had not even given the slightest thought to poor Linda.

Entering the cabin was difficult. Her computer sat on the desk near the window, untouched. Without e-mail, cell phone, and Internet, the solitude was becoming aggravating. She had wanted this outing to be a family holiday, but except for brief moments, it was turning into a scene of separation from her children. Elle sighed while putting on her lavender lotion that would smooth at least her skin if not her soul. The dinner bell interrupted the reverie. She took another deep breath and walked up to dinner at the lodge for the second day.

Most guests were already on the deck. The cocktails, wineglasses, and sparkling waters cluttered the tabletops and the railing. The Ammans were back from their canoe outing, gloating and telling about their heroic descent on some rapids.

"Number twos," Elle heard Amber mutter. "Big deal. I wouldn't even mention it."

PART III

9

Cree

PREPARING FOR THE second day of seminars, Elle donned her camp uniform, which now meant her jeans, T-shirt, and swimsuit. She checked herself in the mirror one last time. The outdoors had begun to get rid of her pallor.

On the way to the lodge, she stopped again at Black Bear. Amber, reclined in one of the armchairs with one of her long legs draped casually over the armrest, was engrossed in her French book. "What do you want, Mom?" she asked with slight irritation. "Josh and Emily are still sleeping."

"Nothing," Elle replied. "I just came by to say good morning." Why was Amber so complicated? Unlike her brother, so fluid and always looking to please others, Amber was blunt and unforgiving. She spoke off the top of her head. Elle held back a comment and, waving a silent good-bye, closed the door behind her.

While following the narrow trail from Whispering Pines up to the lodge, she fumbled in vain for the sunglasses in her bag. Thinking she might have left them in the car, she decided to take the right fork. When she rounded the corner of the lodge, she noticed a bright red

Ford pickup. A young man was leaning against it, deciphering a piece of paper he was holding in his hand. When he heard her approach, he looked up. He was tall and svelte, with jet-black hair that fell loosely over his shoulders.

As Elle came closer, he pulled away from the truck, took a step toward her, and asked, "Are you with the group from *Travel Magazine*?"

When Elle answered affirmatively, he stretched out his hand and with an infectious smile said, "Hi, I'm Cree." After a short hiatus, he added, "I am your guide." The young man, whom Elle judged to be in his mid- to late twenties, was unlike what she had expected. He was quite a contrast to the other older and more rotund members of the Department of Natural Resources. His jeans and black faded T-shirt revealed a lithe, muscular body. His nose was slightly aquiline, and his mouth featured well-formed lips. He stretched out a hand with somewhat delicate-looking long fingers. Elle was riveted to the ground.

"My real name is Pete, Pete Jourdain, but they call me Cree. My mother was Cree. She came from Canada." He smiled and looked at her with dark, piercing eyes in which a small laughing flame seemed to dance.

Elle felt Cree's intense, scrutinizing look. She instantly became aware of the heat and the buzzing of insects. "Well, nice to meet you," she finally managed to say. She cringed as soon as she had uttered the banal words and almost timidly added, "People are probably waiting for us in the seminar room. I came here to look for my sunglasses. I'd better find out if they're in my car."

"I see," Cree answered, his tone slightly mocking. He stepped aside.

She walked past him to her car, which was parked in the shade of the pines. The unexpected encounter was unsettling. She sat in the car for several minutes. The cooler air felt good on her flushed face. Looking straight ahead through the windshield, she noticed the Amman and

Daniels youngsters playing Frisbee on the grass. The ducks were out on their morning waddling stroll at the back of the pond. Elle felt her heart pounding. She tried to regain calm, but to no avail. With shaking knees and fumbling at her sunglasses, she left the car and walked back to the lodge.

Cree was already in the seminar room, talking with the DNR people. Mike signaled to her. "Elle, come and meet our guide, Cree. Actually, his name is Pete, but they call him Cree."

"We just met," she said dryly, nodding in Cree's direction. Cree smiled. Again, Elle was aware of his dazzling smile and of the outline of his body through his T-shirt. Cree was voicing to Tony his concerns about the drought and fire hazards. There had been little rain that year, and water levels were low; brush seemed ready to ignite at any time. Elle could not take her eyes off the young guide. She physically felt his presence in the room and caught only half of his presentation on the state of trees and other plants in the area. She was glad when the ring of the lunch bell helped her snap out of the spell.

The ubiquitous Mike pressed his way toward her at the lunch table. The smell of his aftershave was suddenly nauseating. "So . . . had a good swim this morning?" Mike asked, looking at her inquisitively. "How do you like our guide? Nice-looking fellow." He glanced over at Cree who'd clearly overheard the question and smiled in their direction before turning again to his colleagues.

Elle looked at Cree from her end of the table. His black hair was now pulled back in a ponytail. He leaned forward over his plate while talking to Tony. Elle noticed again his aquiline profile and graceful movements. She heard Mike's voice as if from a distance.

"Are we still on for canoeing at the end of our afternoon session? I can show you the rice beds on the other side of the lake. It will be good practice for our upcoming trip. We'll paddle together into the sunset," he added seductively. "Linda has scheduled a genuine North Woods massage with some lady before dinner."

"Yes, yes, let's do it." Elle nodded distractedly and pitched her fork in the salad.

The afternoon seminar was devoted to wildlife. In a melodious and almost hushed voice, Cree elaborated on the habits of wolves, bears, and eagles as well as pressed on about environmental questions that touched on logging, development, and the impact of climate change. His presence was calm yet intense. John and Tony accompanied Cree's presentations with slides of wildlife, streams, lakes, and rocky islands covered with large pine trees. Elle found a sudden interest in every detail. Spellbound, she could have gone on listening to Cree for hours. But all too soon, chairs were being pushed back; Mike's voice interrupted her daydreaming.

"So how about a quick paddle?" He had not forgotten, and Elle could not refuse. She needed to change and would join Mike down at the dock in half an hour.

She dropped in at Black Bear on her way to Whispering Pines. The children had not yet returned. More clothes and open magazines were covering the floor. The familiar objects in the absence of the children gave her another feeling of foreboding. She quickly retreated.

Back at her own cabin, she changed into her racer suit and threw on a striped T-shirt and black jeans before walking down to the dock, where Mike was waiting. He gave Elle a whistling approval. She smiled, not knowing whether to be openly flattered or to reject him, and that's when she spotted two kayaks coming toward the dock. She recognized Josh and Emily.

10

Josh and Emily

JOSH AND EMILY stretched in the rustic hand-hewn pine bed and, looking deep into each other's eyes, giggled with pure pleasure. All was silent in the cabin. Amber must have left, guessed Emily.

"Hey, Emily, how about a little kayaking?" Josh asked her while stroking her ringlets. "Canoeing is lame. It's for old folks. Kayaking will be more exciting. Let's grab some quick breakfast and see if we can get a couple of kayaks and a lunch from the lodge."

They quickly rose and hurried up to the main building. Breakfast was over, and Marge, Betsy, and Ruth were already cleaning up. Using his innate charm, Josh convinced the women to offer their young guests a couple of blueberry muffins and what had come to be known among the guests as some of "the brew" that Tom and Jennie stubbornly referred to as "their coffee."

Laughing, Betsy, already clearly quite taken by Josh, ambled into the kitchen to prepare a lunch for him and Emily. Having cleared the kayaks with Tom, the pair went back to Black Bear to put on their gear. Emily carefully anointed herself with her ultimate sunscreen—SPF

50. She proudly read the label aloud. "The sun won't damage my skin. I hate wrinkles. I'd hate to look old."

In spite of their mannerisms and their movie-star looks, they were both athletic. Setting out from the wooden pier, they paddled side by side with ease, their yellow-and-red kayaks moving swiftly through the placid waters toward the eastern part of the wilderness lake, out of which flowed a small river that, Tom Silver had informed them, connected with a larger lake farther north. "Let's follow the creek up to the other lake," Emily suggested. Paddling north—that is, downstream, they shot a couple of small rapids and soon felt exhilarated under the sun and amid the white waters. In the distance, Emily noticed a small black shape swimming across the river.

"Look, a lost dog! Let's bring him back."

"It's a bear, duh," Josh corrected her, laughing heartily.

"A bear!" Emily joined in Josh's laughter. "A real teddy bear? Oh, he looks so cuddly."

"Don't try to hug him. Bears have big claws." Josh made a scratching gesture and a deep growling sound.

"Just like you, sweetie," Emily laughed. Teddy had by now disappeared into the bushes on the opposite shore. This ended their conversation momentarily.

When they spotted a large reddish boulder, Josh suggested that they pause there for lunch. They pulled their kayaks onto a small sandy area and unloaded their food. "I'm dying for a swim," exclaimed Emily. They hopped off the rock and into the clear running waters. "I hope there are no beavers here. Marge, Betsy, and Ruth told me to be careful. If not, we cry beaver ho!"

Josh laughed. "Very funny!"

They splashed and chased each other. Hoisting themselves up near a submerged rock in the middle of the stream, they let the silvery water run over them. Emily screeched with delight. Their hair was blowing in the wind. Wet strands stuck to their foreheads. Their catalog looks were a bit rumpled. Josh put his arms around Emily's waist suggestively.

"Josh," Emily cooed, "don't do that." But she could not resist. She turned around. They looked into each other's eyes again. "Isn't that what couples do in the movies?" Emily laughed. The magic worked. They felt their youthful passion surge up in them with all its might.

Without a word, they emerged from the waters still holding hands and started kissing on the rock. Soon they lay in each other's embrace while the hot August sun bore down on them. The world started to vacillate. They were oblivious to their surroundings, except to each other's breathing and to the heat emanating from the dark red rock.

"Oh, Josh!" sweet Emily exhaled when she came back to the world. "I love you. I missed you so much all year."

"I love you too," Josh replied with his poster smile. "I feel so good with you. I never want to be separated again." They became serious and lay in silence for a few moments. An eagle muttered in the distance. The leaves of the nearby aspen trees rustled in the midday breeze. Except for a few sounds of nature, all was perfectly still. Their animal instincts took over again.

"Let's have lunch before a bear gets to it," Josh said a short time later. He inspected the lunch bag that Betsy had so carefully prepared for them. "Ham sandwiches, my favorite." He popped open a can of soda.

"The Diet Coke is for me," Emily pleaded. "You won't like me if I'm fat." Emily was clearly back in her media world.

Josh protested gallantly, "I will always love you, regardless of your weight."

"That's not true. Look, I already have ripples here." She pointed to her upper thighs.

They ate quietly. Then their joking mood returned. "Wow, isn't it something to make love in the great outdoors?" Josh said. They laughed comfortably together. "In Mother Nature's embrace ..."

"It sure feels different with the hard rocks under you." They laughed some more and then looked at each other longingly and resumed kissing. After their second turn at lovemaking, the conversation changed course.

"I'm so glad that we won't be separated next year." Emily was alluding to the fact that she was starting college barely a hundred miles from Josh. "We can at least be together on weekends. How do girls dress at your school? Do I have to wear Prada to be respected?"

Josh reassured her with a laugh. "No, come on. Only the devil wears Prada. Everyone wears jeans. It's casual—except for formals."

"Oh, I can't wait for the formal. I already know what I'm going to wear. I'll have my hair done and everything. It will be so cool ... How do you think your Mom is doing?" Emily inquired, abruptly changing the subject. "She still looks sad."

"Yeah," said Josh, looking away. "She took the divorce hard, you know. Dad was such a jerk. He accuses Amber and me of siding with her. We didn't do anything. He's the one who just moved out. Mom came here to be with us but also to forget. She'll be okay. I hope she'll meet someone else soon. Let's go," he said, suddenly in a bad mood.

"Oh no," said Emily, reaching out for Josh's hand. "I didn't mean to make you mad."

"It's not you," answered Josh. "It's my dad. He is such a shit. Let's go back."

They pushed their kayaks back into the water. Paddling upstream was a little harder. "Perfect for digesting your lunch," grumbled Emily. "Let's race," she exclaimed. They paddled as fast as they could and arrived at the mouth of the river exhausted. Josh barely beat Emily by half a boat length.

"Pretty tough lady," Josh remarked, admiring his companion's stamina. They pushed their kayaks through a rocky area and then headed west on the lake as the sun was nearing the tree line.

"Look, Josh, we're paddling into the sunset," said Emily with a grin. "How romantic."

They were approaching the pier of Loon Lodge just as Elle and Mike emerged from the trees. "Josh, isn't that your mom?" Emily asked.

"Yeah, sure looks like her," Josh replied, squinting his eyes.

"She's with that guy," Emily objected.

"Okay. She should have some fun."

"But he's here with another woman."

Josh shrugged his shoulders. "She can take care of herself." His fowl mood had returned.

As they were coming ashore with their kayaks, they looked intently at Elle and Mike. "Hey, Mom, what's up?" Josh called from a short distance.

"Hello, kids. Did you have a good time?" Elle had a trace of guilt in her voice.

"We're not children, you know," Josh corrected his mother, "but it was awesome. We saw a bear and a couple of eagles. We had some choice swims. Emily is a great kayaker."

"Oh, get off it, Josh," Emily crooned.

"Are you guys sailing into the sunset?" Josh finally asked his mother.

"Yeah," Mike said with a grin. "I'm taking your mother to the rock across the lake. I'll show her the rice beds. Nothing to worry about; she'll be in good hands."

11

Mike and Elle

MIKE TOSSED A couple of life jackets and paddles into one of the lodge's green Old Town canoes, signaled that Elle should climb in the bow, and pushed them off. They glided along, Mike paddling and steering from the stern. A family of ducks fluttered ahead of them. An occasional fish rose to the surface in the hope of catching an insect. "So, Lady E," as Mike had begun to call Elle, "how do you like this guide? Pretty handsome guy, huh?" With these words, the magic of the silence was interrupted.

Startled, Elle wondered what Mike meant by his blunt question. Had he observed how flustered she was by the young guide's presence, though the latter did not seem to realize anything? In fact, Cree paid no more attention to her than to the others in the group. Elle did not want anyone—including Mike and, even more so, Cree—to become aware of her emotions.

"You like him?" Mike seemed to be probing with a mix of real curiosity and perhaps even a pang of jealousy. "Older women and younger men; it's quite the thing," he needled.

The tone of the conversation soured on Elle. "Mike, please," she said meekly. "I'm here on an assignment, just like you."

He laughed. "Yeah, sure." However, he clearly thought it wise not to pursue in this direction. They continued in a quiet punctuated by the swoosh of the paddles and an occasional thud when Elle's paddle clumsily hit the side of the canoe.

After reaching the far shore, they beached the canoe at the foot of a high outcropping from where they could look down on the rice beds. Mike offered Elle his hand, and helping her out of the tippy watercraft, he glanced at her sideways. She pretended not to notice. They struggled up the steep embankment so they could look out over the rice beds. Sitting on top of the large boulder and looking across the glassy lake, they guessed where the lodge was better than they saw it. Occasionally, the sun lit up one of the windowpanes.

"Quite a group we have! Quite an adventure! I wonder what will come of it." The setting sun disposed Mike toward philosophizing while he continued to scrutinize Elle. He took out a silver hip flask. "Care for some bourbon? It's Knob Creek. My favorite."

Elle usually stayed away from hard liquor, but given her state of mind that day, she accepted. Mike poured a shot in the top of the flask, thereby converting it into a shot glass. They sat facing the lake that in the evening light looked as if it were on fire. Tiny waves lapped at the rocks beneath them.

"Quite a spectacle," commented Mike, who always liked to put everything into simple words.

"Yes," she murmured. The calm of the evening scene was not entirely capable of quieting her inner turmoil.

Despite the bourbon and the serenity of the surroundings, she was still agitated and only gradually became aware of Mike's voice. "So what's eating you up inside? Looks like you're really in a state." Behind his gruff airs, Mike was clearly a shrewd reader of people, and his taking a liking to Elle was obvious.

She turned to him and smiled. "Mike, as I already told you, the divorce turned my life upside down. I don't really feel like talking about it. I came here to forget. I thought it would do the kids and me a lot of good to be together as a family."

"How did it happen?" Mike persisted. "Did *he* run away?" She nodded. "What a fool. From a lady like you! Many men would give a fortune to be with you."

"Well, that wasn't my ex-husband's case."

"So you don't want romance? Do you think you're on a family holiday here? Look at your kids. They're almost grown. You want to keep them back so you won't be alone?"

Mike was right. Since their arrival, Elle was becoming painfully aware of the discrepancy between her imagination and reality. She was hoping to reconnect with her teenage children. The truth of the matter was that the children were devoted to her, yet they did have their lives to live. Josh was quite settled with Emily. Amber seemed to be embarking on a summer romance with Lyle, who followed her like a puppy and whose advances were too blatant to be overlooked. Yet she continued to surveil her mother and had already dropped several hints about Mike.

Over the last few days, Elle could not get *Bonjour Tristesse*, the novel that Amber was reading, out of her mind. When she had read it in school, Elle, who was then Amber's age and that of the daughter in the story, completely identified with the latter. Now, twenty years later, she was rather on the side of the father's lover. The daughter was really the one who meddled in the adults' lives. Why was this old story haunting her simply because Amber was reading it? She was not exactly on the French Riviera—only a wilderness lake—and no man except for Mike had openly made signs, though he was technically taken. Cree's smiling face flashed through her mind. Cree? No, she tried to convince herself, he was too young and didn't pay any more attention to her than to anyone else. He was polite but distant. Yet Elle could not shake a funny feeling that had taken hold of her.

Mike poured a little more bourbon. "Care for another?" He seemed surprised when Elle nodded. She emptied the content of the shot glass in one big gulp. "Hey, Lady E, that's more like it," he said with admiration.

The sun had now disappeared behind the tree line in the west, and the sky had turned dark red. Mike moved over and put his arm around Elle's shoulders. He leaned toward her and started kissing her. She let it happen for a while but then pushed him off and rose quickly. "No, Mike. Think of Linda. Besides, I can't be with anyone yet."

Mike sat looking somewhat dumbfounded and disappointed. It was apparent that he had hoped for a little more from this outing. However, in gentlemanly fashion, he refrained this time from putting his disappointment into words. "Time to go, then," he said abruptly. "Dinner will be served before we even get back. Linda is going to be in a state. It will undo the benefit of her massage."

They paddled back in silence. The first stars appeared in the darkening sky. The lights of the lodge that flickered between the trees in the distance helped guide them. It was already night when they reached the dock. Only myriad stars and the moon, soon to be full, lit the waters.

It was not Linda but Amber who greeted them at the end of the dock, sitting in one of the Adirondack chairs. "Mom, what took you so long? Where have you been?" She sounded almost threatening as she voiced her displeasure. "Dinner is already done. I kept you some and put it in your cabin."

Elle quickly thanked Mike, who disappeared into the darkness en route to his cabin, and followed Amber up to Whispering Pines.

"Mom, I told you, no hanky-panky," Amber said while walking.

In vain, Elle tried to reassure her daughter.

12

A Nature Hike

AT SUNRISE, ELLE made her way down to the lake, half expecting to see Mike, who did not show. Had she offended him? Wondering, she made her way into the calm waters. She was beginning to like the sensuous side of swimming in a lake. Through the rising mist, she glanced pockets of deep blue sky. The morning sun was casting long oblique rays through the trees behind her. The shore where she had sat with Mike the previous evening was already in full sunlight. Elle dove into the clear reddish lake and slowly swam out toward the deep. Kicking water high up in the air, she watched myriad droplets sparkle in the early morning light. A sudden feeling of pleasure overcame her. Elle let it spread through her limbs before swimming back to shore. Humming a tune, she rubbed herself vigorously with her red bath towel. What prompted this sudden feeling of almost happiness? Her new surroundings? The anticipation of Mike? Or, perhaps, of Cree?

By the time she arrived in the dining hall, everyone was seated. "Hey, Elle, overslept?" asked Tony. "Next time I'll come and knock on your door." Mike waved but seemed distant. The DNR people were sitting by themselves, engrossed in local gossip. Only Cree had not yet arrived. Elle deplored his absence but quickly checked herself. *Don't be foolish,* she admonished herself. internally. She sat down with her new colleagues and, sipping coffee and chewing on a slice of Jenny's bread, listened to their conversations. Suddenly, in the frame of the sliding doors opening out onto the deck, Cree appeared. He wore a simple gray T-shirt and jeans with another red bandana around his neck. Against the light, his body seemed even trimmer.

"Hey, Cree, it took you a while," Tony greeted the latecomer. "Overslept like Elle?"

Cree laughed and cast a quick glance toward Elle, who felt a shooting sensation in her body. Alleging that he'd had work to finish, he poured himself a cup of coffee and sat down at the end of Elle's table. She found his smile even more dazzling than on the previous day; it was utterly disarming. Was it studied or did it come naturally? His eyes cast a glance around the dining room before uttering some words that resembled a muffled hello. "Everyone's well and ready?" he added. Beneath the smile, Elle thought she perceived a fleeting sign of tension. It quickly left his face, which was again as smooth as the surface of the lake this morning.

"So, Cree, where do you live?" Mike, the more inquisitive of the group, inquired.

"In town, forty or so miles away." Cree seemed somewhat vague.

"You're going to come on our first hike with us?" Mike continued.

"Of course. I'm your guide. Today we'll explore one of the nearby trails."

"How about getting started?" Tony said. "It will take us a good while to drive to the head of the trail to park our van."

Elle rushed back to her cabin to outfit herself for her first walk in the woods. She checked herself in the mirror. Her tanned face looked thinner. Her large gray eyes shined brighter. The dark circles seemed to be disappearing. She looked at this stranger in the mirror and paused. She mused about her mundane and, in retrospect, rather empty life. In a flash, she thought about what it had been and wondered with trepidation how it would unfold. Mike was right. They all had embarked on an adventure together. Where would it take her?

She quickly grabbed a trail jacket—Tony had told them the day before always to take some long-sleeved outerwear in case of mosquitoes, which the visitors and the locals alike referred to as the "state birds." She slung her backpack over her shoulder and headed up to the parking lot. The DNR minivan was ready to go, with the rest of the team already seated inside.

"Elle, squeeze in here," Mike called out, offering to move over.

Elle had just taken a step toward the van when she heard a voice behind her say, "Come with me; I have room." She turned abruptly and found herself face-to-face with Cree, who was just descending the wooden steps in the back of the lodge. He nodded in the direction of his red pickup, which was parked in the shade of the trees.

Elle gestured to Mike. "We'll catch up with you guys. Thanks for the offer anyhow. I'll ride with Cree."

It was the first time she'd pronounced his name aloud. *Cree.* It had a funny sound. In French, she mused, it meant to create and even to believe.

Cree hopped into his truck and opened the passenger door for Elle. She stepped up and strapped herself into the black seat. The beige minivan took off down the winding road. Cree followed with Elle. When they reached the intersection, Cree pointed out the large white pine on the other side of the county road.

"A first-growth white pine, over two hundred years old. The entire region was covered with them before they were cut down at the beginning of the last century." He fell silent.

Once they had reached the open road, the minivan disappeared in a cloud of dust. Cree followed at a distance. "Care for some music?" he asked. Elle shook her head. "I also like to drive in silence." He rolled down the windows. The hot air streamed in. Even in midday, Elle could hear the crickets. Cree pointed out the peculiar, almost acrid, smell of the North Woods. "It's the aspens," he explained. Elle breathed in the smells before she leaned back in her seat while trying not to show her excitement.

Cree was a steady driver, his hands bearing a solid grip on the wheel. He looked straight ahead at the road, keeping his distance from the van so as not to be caught in its dust or flying rocks. At times, he took a quick glance out the window at the passing scenery. Now and again, Elle cast him a sidelong glance. In spite of his age, he seemed calm and assured. She followed the lines of his profile and again noticed his thin well-formed lips. Something was stirring, though she was still reluctant to acknowledge what the turmoil might be.

Underneath his red bandana, Elle noticed a necklace holding a pendant. What was its meaning? She was studying him intensely when Cree suddenly turned toward her. Elle was startled. Did he notice her reaction? Cree looked at her straight on, slightly squinting his eyes. His eyes were sparkling, yet at the same time, she thought she saw a dark fire burning deep in them, visible only in a certain light. Like right now, in the car. Despite his composure, Cree seemed to be a passionate person. His intensity attracted and at times, like right now, almost scared her a little. He smiled at her, revealing his glistening white teeth.

"We haven't really gotten acquainted," he said. "So tell me, what brings you here? Why this project?"

"Oh," she said with a sigh, "that's a long story. I came here to forget."

"Forget about what?"

"Oh, things that happened to me ..." she said vaguely.

Cree looked at Elle fixedly. "I see," he said after a slight pause. "To forget, you know, you have to forget about yourself. You have to learn to look at the world and to love it. This is the perfect spot for it. This kind of landscape will help you get over aches and pains of the body and the soul." He gestured with his free hand. "It surrounds you and overwhelms you with its smells, its sounds, and its colors. It will pull you out of yourself." Elle let the words sink in. Cree looked straight ahead at the road again.

"Yeah, beautiful countryside," she managed to say, chastising herself again for the banality of her own words.

"Yes, it is. Must have been even more so before the settlers came." Cree became somber. Elle would come to learn that in addition to his dedication to the environment, Cree identified with the Native American community on many issues. "It's a great place but a fragile environment that is easily disturbed," he added.

They fell silent. Again, Elle became aware of the heat and the general hum of the insects. Cree was first to speak.

"Are you widowed? Divorced?"

"Divorced," Elle answered feebly, this time looking straight ahead.

"It happens," Cree said. "Do you miss him?"

"Not really," she blurted out. She wanted to add "especially not right now—in your company," but she bit her tongue.

"Sometimes relations ..." Cree again gesticulated and broke off. "So what do you do during the year?"

"I teach," she answered.

"I see. What subject?"

Elle explained her position at Lincoln University and said that she came here truly to forget but also to be with her children.

"I see. The part about your forgetting is okay; as for the children, you need them more than they need you." Cree scrutinized Elle again. "You have to figure out how to be on your own and not to live through them."

She felt ashamed. "How about you?" she asked in an effort to change the course of the conversation.

"Oh, me ... I'm working in town right now for a lawyer, and in the summer, I'm also working for the DNR and guiding as much as I can. I finished college five years ago and am interested in conservation and sustainability. My dream is to apply to law school, but ..." Cree became serious again and his voice trailed off. "And you?" he asked Elle, changing the subject in turn. "Will you go back to the city?"

"Oh, yes. I have my teaching job, you know, and my research projects." Elle sighed.

Cree again looked her straight in the eye. "You have to take hold of yourself," he finally declared. "You have to go outside of yourself and reconnect with the world, wherever you are. I'll say it again: this setting will be perfect."

"Yeah," Elle exhaled. Cree's words hit her to the quick. The image of Max flashed through her mind again. He had never talked to her this way. How different it was with Cree, yet he was so young. "You're very easy to talk to, you know," she found heard herself saying almost involuntarily.

Cree looked slightly surprised. "So are you." He nodded after a brief pause, though without a smile. Elle felt a spark igniting between the two. The quiet returned, but something, she thought, had changed. For the next fifteen minutes, Elle lived in a different time and space. When they arrived at the trail's head, she was truly disappointed.

*　　*　　*

They started their trek in single file along a corduroy path built across a mossy peat bog. Cree, Tony, and Sherry explained its delicate ecology. They pointed out flesh-eating plants, black spruces, a scrubby indigenous tree, and the glorious tamaracks that dropped their needles in the fall after they turned bright yellow. Joan and Jim gathered tiny plant specimens. Without ever looking the least bit ruffled in spite of the heat, Rod and Brett moved about swiftly, clicking their cameras. Mike made Linda nervous by continuously bantering about wild animals. They climbed through rocky areas with oversized boulders deposited by a distant glacier age. Elle looked at them in awe, wondering where she would escape if they started rolling. The spruces and tamaracks gave way to jack pines, the gnarly tall conifer that reseeded itself best through fire, when the heat made its cones explode. Cree told them how fires were crucial to regenerating the vegetation of the area. He invited them to study dried up animal scats, which prompted them to imagine wolves howling from the ridges on cold winter nights.

From the rear of the group, Elle watched Cree's measured, even gait. While the others stumbled over roots and branches, he calmly moved ahead. Wiping droplets of sweat off his forehead, Mike spoke wryly about the price they all paid for the privilege to sweat and toil. They climbed over large tree trunks, especially aspen, downed by a recent windstorm. If the trunks were barring the road, jumping over them was no more arduous than exercising at the gym. If the crown of the tree happened to be on the path as well, the challenge was greater. With his axe, Tony chopped off the larger branches, and Cree held back some of the smaller ones so the rest of the group could pass. When Elle slipped, he held out his arm to prevent her from falling. With embarrassment, she meekly uttered a few inaudible words of thanks. Cree smiled. Elle felt undone. Did Cree notice anything?

At a large wilderness lake, they found a campsite furnished with a weathered picnic table and collapsed onto its benches. With a last effort, Mike gathered some kindling and built a fire in the designated pit. "Who wants marshmallows?" he asked jovially.

Tony told them that the swimming was safe, so Elle decided it was worth a try. It might relieve not only her aching limbs but also calm down her overwrought nerves. Though she was no longer afraid of strange creatures surging from the depths of lakes, Elle felt queasy; still, she wanted to show off in front of Cree.

When she made it back to shore, the group was sitting around singing praises for the lodge's tasty sandwiches. Mike was roasting his marshmallows. "Just like back in grade school," he exclaimed. When Elle stepped out of the water, she felt all eyes upon her, including Cree's, who seemed to look right through her impassively. Tony whistled.

"Quite a sight in the wilderness," Mike joked again. His words made Elle cringe, but at the same time, she began to find an unexpected pleasure in allowing herself to be seen.

Having donned her jeans and T-shirt, Elle sat down, her wet hair hanging over her shoulders. "You look like a teenager," Mike noted. "And," he added in a lower tone, "you act like one too." Elle was flushed. What did he mean? Was Mike aware of her turmoil?

They sat huddled together on the benches of the weathered picnic table with carved-out hearts pierced with arrows and accompanied by names. Mike deciphered the hieroglyphics aloud. "Marge and Andy ... Bill and Meg ... The beauty of true love," he added, looking in the direction of Elle, who kept silent.

She reached for a piece of fruit in the middle of the table at the same moment that Cree made the same gesture from the opposite side. Their hands touched for a split second. Elle's heart raced. Cree laughed. Did he even discern that she blushed? *This is silly,* she chided herself. *Mike is right. You're behaving like a teenager, worse than your daughter. Act your age.*

As she made herself sit up straight, Cree looked at her and laughed. He might have been laughing at Mike's joke. Or was he laughing at her? Or laughing *with* her? *How stupid of me!* Elle tried to put the thought out of her mind.

Their picnic ended with fresh coffee that Sherry had brewed over the fire. It far surpassed, they all agreed, any latte from the city. Elle wished that lunch could last forever, but all too soon, Tony and Cree put out the fire and gave the signal to head on.

Elle made sure to trail far behind Cree so he could not help her over more fallen logs. Cree was right. She needed to get hold of herself. Her thoughts were diverted by the attention she had to give to the moss-covered rocks and the large roots on the path that led up a steep hill offering grand vistas onto countless lakes and endless forests. At the head of yet another shimmering lake, a large field spiked with tree trunks that looked like mushroom cones indicated the presence of beavers. The animals had successfully damned up the little rivulet. Several generations of them had produced a good-sized marsh dotted with rotting tree trunks.

"Beaver ho!" Mike exclaimed with a laugh.

Cree explained that it was too early. As nocturnal creatures, beavers did not come out until dusk.

It was already getting dark when they completed their loop and reached the gravel road where the van and Cree's truck were parked. Elle did not volunteer to drive with her guide. His proximity in the cab would have been unbearable. She climbed into the van while Sherry nonchalantly joined Cree.

Elle sat next to Mike. The drive made her drowsy, and after watching the mist rise from the moonlit marshes bordered by the jagged outline of black spruces, she dozed off. When she woke, they were at the lodge. She had been sleeping on Mike's shoulder.

"Well, Lady E," he said in a mocking, seductive tone, "glad to be of assistance."

How nice it was to sleep on another shoulder, Elle thought dreamily as she disembarked with the others. Cree had dropped off Sherry and was still standing near his truck. When Elle filed by him, she had the fleeting impression that he was beckoning her. Her heart pounding, she stopped in front of him.

"How did you like your first hike?" he asked. Elle hoped that in the darkness and with only the light that came from the lodge, Cree did not see her turn crimson. She searched for words and finally could muster only a nervous laugh.

13

Amber and Lyle

AFTER HER MOTHER left in Cree's truck, Amber stewed in a sullen state of mind. She stomped back into the empty dining hall. Still brooding, she poked around her plate of half-eaten blueberry pancakes. Lyle tried to convince her one more time to join him on a combined bike ride and hike.

"They have amazing trails here. Real choice! We can ride over to Big Lake and then hike up to a ridge from where we'll have a really cool view into Canada. I did it with my parents before you guys arrived."

Amber remained silent. Then, unexpectedly, she consented. Lyle turned purple with joy. He gave Amber a big hug.

"Okay!" he cried as his glasses fogged up. "I'll get the bikes. I'll ask Marge, Betsy, and Ruth to fix us a picnic."

"Don't stress yourself," retorted Amber condescendingly. "I'm first going back to the cabin. I want to do some reading. See you in an hour." Amber pushed her chair back, haughtily strutting out of the dining hall. Lyle, in ecstasy, followed her slender silhouette with his eyes.

Amber returned to Black Bear. Josh and Emily had already departed for yet another kayaking expedition. Why was it always her brother who was lucky? What was it with him? Why did she get stuck with Lyle? And now her mother was running around with these two guys, especially Cree, who seemed to have made quite an impression on her. Cree! Why her mother and not her, after all? Amber stomped in rage, but then, in a sudden reversal, decided to shake off her crisis and read another page of *Bonjour Tristesse*.

She took it up when Cecile, the girl in the story, had found a really cool guy. And all she had was Lyle. She was flattered by his attention, but he should not ever believe that she was attracted to him. Amber continued reading. Cecile was becoming increasingly irritated by the presence of her father's lover. The new woman spent too much time with the father while setting up rules for his daughter. Amber abruptly closed the book. Nobody was laying down the law for her. These two guys around her mother were simply no good. Not that she needed her mother that much, but when she wanted her, she had to be available. In any case, she should not be involved with these men. Mike was yuck, and Cree was too young.

An hour later to the second, Lyle knocked on the door. "Okay, Amber, let's go." When he tried to touch her arm, Amber recoiled. She was still sulking.

"Leave me alone."

"Oh, Amber, I'm so sorry. I didn't want to make you mad. Look here. I got the lunches all packed and the bikes ready."

"Okay. Wait for me up at the parking lot," Amber finally said. Lyle left, pulling the door closed behind him. Amber remained motionless. At last, she combed her hair into a ponytail and pulled it through the back of her White Sox cap. Armed with a pair of aviator glasses and after a last look in the mirror, she headed up the trail.

Lyle, who was waiting, was clearly ecstatic when he saw her climb the path. He had signed out two mountain bikes and had packed the lunches in his North Face backpack. "I'll show you the way. Let's go down the main road. Then we'll pedal east for about ten miles to the Big Lake Trail. We'll hike up a high ridge and have some lunch."

They took off. "Let's race down to the big pine!" shouted Amber. From the lodge, they sped down the winding path through the tall pine trees until they reached the county road. Amber who was fiercely competitive beat Lyle by over a foot. Stopping at the intersection in spite of Amber's snide comments about "real heavy traffic," Lyle commented on the large white pine across the road.

"My dad says it's a first-growth tree. It must be two hundred years old," he said in a clear attempt to show off his new knowledge.

"I know," was Amber's laconic answer. "My mom already told me. My brother calls it dead man's tree."

They continued pedaling swiftly down the winding gravel road along streams, swamps, and forest. Several pickup trucks passed them. Each time, the dust billowed so thickly that they had to stop. "Some kind of fun!" sneered Amber. "Reminds me of a windstorm in the Sahara!" Finally, they arrived at the head of the trail.

"Let's lock the bikes to a tree and hide them," he said. "From here, we'll have to hike in. They don't allow bikes in the Boundary Waters."

"That's lame," commented Amber as Lyle tied the bikes to a couple of pine trees.

They started hiking along a narrow trail, through tall grass, stumbling over hidden rocks, climbing over fallen spruces and aspen, scratching their arms and legs on twigs and thorns. Lyle gallantly held the branches out of Amber's way. Amber played independent and rejected his help. They hopped on rocks to cross a couple of rivulets before they arrived at a good-sized creek.

"Looks like we have to swim across this one," Amber grumbled.

"Oh, I can carry you," exclaimed Lyle in anticipation.

"Yeah, really," answered Amber ironically. "I can handle it." She stepped fearlessly into the murky waters, followed by Lyle. The water reached well above their knees.

"Oh, look! There's a beaver lodge down there too. Wouldn't that be fun if they swam after us and bit our legs?" Lyle joked.

"Some picnic you had in mind." Lyle laughed nervously, seeming confused as to whether she was serious or merely playing. They continued their ascent until, at long last, they reached the top of a ridge from where, even Amber had to admit, they did have an amazing view. Forests and lakes with small rocky pine-covered islands stretched as far as the eye could see.

They sat down on the soft moss-covered rocky plateau warmed by the sun and leaned against the trunk of a fallen pine tree. Lyle grabbed the lunch from his backpack.

"Look, eggs. I love hard-boiled eggs!" he exclaimed. "They even included mayonnaise."

Amber mocked him. "Why, did you never have a school lunch?"

"Oh, and turkey sandwiches!" Lyle continued, unperturbed. Famished by their trek and the great outdoors, Amber abruptly stopped her sneering to tackle her sandwich with a healthy appetite. For a while, she overcame her feistiness and shared in the meal and the beauty of their surroundings.

Made drowsy by the food and the midday sun, they fell silent. From the corner of his eyes, Lyle watched Amber, who stared straight ahead as if she had some strange fascination with the distant horizon. After visibly hesitating and even indulging in some fake coughing, Lyle drew near Amber and began to kiss her.

Perhaps, in the warmth of the sunlight, Amber was, for a moment, under the spell of his seduction. Or she was simply pretending. She wasn't even sure she knew herself. Lyle's timid hands finally began to touch Amber's body and moved slowly up her arms and toward her breasts. Amber let it happen, though she continued to look straight into the distance. Even when Lyle gently pushed her down on the ground, she did not object. Then, all of a sudden, she moved abruptly and pushed her hapless suitor back.

"Lyle, please," she said rather sternly.

"Amber, I didn't want to offend you."

"You aren't offending me. I just don't want to do it. Besides," she added defiantly, "I don't love you. Let's just forget it. This is pathetic."

Lyle was visibly shaken by this sudden reversal of fortune, but his attraction for Amber had the upper hand. "Oh, Amber, I'm so sorry. I thought you wanted me to ... to kiss you. What did I do wrong?"

"Oh, get lost. You're not a man. Let's just get home, okay?"

Plainly crestfallen, Lyle packed the remainder of the food, and without another word, they started the long trek down the hill.

When Amber and Lyle arrived back at the lodge, her mother was nowhere in sight. Amber spent a sullen dinner with Lyle and the other guests. She could hardly involve herself in Lyle's checker game and rushed to the door when she heard the sound of an engine. She saw her mother and the group disembark from the van. In the light shining from the lodge, Amber noticed her mother laughing nervously while engaged in conversation with Cree. The two appeared to be in a rather intimate pose. Her mother certainly looked seductive all of a sudden.

Determined, Amber walked past the group and, after brushing off Mike's greetings with an abrupt gesture of the hand, went straight to her mother. "Hi, Mom," she said, feigning cheeriness. "How was your trip? Do you want me to show you what we brought back from our hike?"

"What is it? Can I see?" Elle replied.

Amber could hear the fake interest in her mother's voice. "Oh, no, not here. In our cabin. Come with me."

Looking reluctant, Elle followed her daughter. Amber thought she heard her sigh. She looked triumphantly at Cree as she walked past him to take her mother back to her cabin.

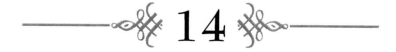

14

Canoeing with Cree

THAT NIGHT, ELLE dreamed of walking on a narrow path along a steep precipice. At the bottom of the rocky cliff, the swollen waters of a creek spilled over large boulders. Elle was on the verge of losing her balance and tried in vain to steady herself. In the distance, she saw Cree disappear behind a wall of fire. She awoke with her heart racing.

Outside, she heard the plaintive hoot of an owl. *Hoo, hoo-hoo!* She rose and opened the window, listening to the eerie sound until it faded in the night. The moon had set, but through the branches of the trees, she glimpsed the nocturnal sky, which was sprinkled with stars. The fresh air carried a faint scent of pines into the room. Elle returned to her solitary bed but could not get Cree off her mind. She clearly saw his face and heard the sound of his melodious voice with that naggingly peculiar inflection that went with his description of the elusive wolves, the life of bears, and the soothing qualities of medicinal plants. She also remembered how Amber had stared at Cree with a mixture of awe and utter contempt. It was already getting light when Elle fell into a heavy sleep.

A few hours later, a loud knock on the door made her bolt upright. "Who is it?"

"It's me, Amber." Elle threw on her robe and hastened to open the door.

Amber pushed her way into the room, past her mother. "They are again waiting for you at breakfast," Amber said with a tone of reproach. "Where have you been?"

"Right here ... sleeping," Elle answered with fake calm. "I didn't really go to sleep until the early-morning hours."

Amber looked around the cabin as if looking for evidence, not uttering another word for a moment or two. "Okay," she finally said dryly, like a detective. "I'd better be going. Lyle wants me to go kayaking with him down some whitewater river. Be back for dinner. You stay out of mischief," she added, looking sternly at her mother. With these words, she exited the cabin and slammed the door.

Amber's abrupt departure, her enigmatic words, and the anticipation of spending a day in the company of Cree all contributed to Elle's state of agitation. She dressed while mulling over her thoughts. In the distance, she heard the now-familiar noises of the lodge. A volley of laughter traveled all the way to her cabin—it must be Betsy—and car doors slammed.

Distractedly, she climbed up the steep path and entered the lodge through the sliding doors of the deck, catching a glimpse of Cree. She stopped abruptly. Her heart was beating so violently that she was sure everyone in the room could hear it pound. Cree was standing at one of the tables next to Tony. When he turned around and saw Elle, he gave her one of his signature smiles. A sudden shyness overcame her. She had to pinch herself before being able to utter a meek hello, and then she helped herself to breakfast and sat down at the only empty seat, which was opposite Cree.

"So, Elle, have you been writing? Is that why you're late?" Cree inquired.

"Oh, well, no, I haven't really started yet. Anyhow, you know, it's always a struggle," she added feebly. "Words don't always come easily …" She shifted uncomfortably in her chair.

"Don't bother Lady E. Remember, she came here to forget," intervened Mike. "Don't give her a hard time."

Elle was uncomfortable. "Don't listen to Mike," she replied almost bashfully.

Cree laughed and, noticing her distress, changed the topic. "Are you all looking forward to our trip?"

"I can't wait," Elle heard herself say. "I'm afraid I won't be much good, though. I don't really know how to canoe." Elle felt conflicted, struggling against her own attraction to this young man while trying vainly to persuade herself that she should not give in. Yet Cree's attention was not only flattering like Mike's his presence also stirred something else in her, something that had been dormant for years. Max had never really asked her questions. He simply told her what to do. They had established this routine early on in their marriage, and for eighteen years, it had seemed to work. Cree, she convinced herself, was more attuned to other people's needs. He was a keen listener. When he noticed her disquiet, he changed the subject.

That day, Elle was even more enraptured with the seminar, especially when it was Cree's turn to hold forth on the art of ricing. At the end of the afternoon session, as they were leaving the room, Cree told Elle that if she wanted, he would take her to one of the nearby rivers for a quick canoe ride. He would show her the rice beds and teach her how to canoe. She hesitated.

"Are you too busy?" Cree asked abruptly, in a tone that betrayed a feeling of being slighted.

"No, it's just … Oh well, yes, let's do it. I'll meet you in fifteen minutes," she blurted out. She hurried back to Whispering Pines and opened the window wide to let the breeze in. She needed air. The thought of going canoeing with Cree was overwhelming. She finally composed herself to the point where she was able to grab a sweatshirt, and then she quickly raced back up to the parking lot.

Cree had already loaded a canoe and was waiting for her in his truck with the passenger door wide open. Elle gingerly climbed into the cab. He revved the engine and they were off. Feeling exhilarated like a little girl, she watched the lodge disappear behind a cloud of dust. Cree was again holding the steering wheel with a light but steady grip. She looked at him coyly. His profile stood out against the sunlight. She followed the line of his high forehead to his fine aquiline nose, finally lingering on his lips. Cree wore his usual bandana around the neck and a faded black T-shirt. Half hidden by the bandana, Elle noticed the same necklace with a pendant. She wondered about its meaning but kept silent.

Cree initiated the conversation. He wanted to know more about her work and seemed interested in her writings on urban problems. As for Elle, she overcame some of her bashfulness and inquired further about Cree. He had grown up in the area. His mother was a Cree. She passed away when he was a toddler, and his father remarried. He often felt that he lived between two cultures. He cared about the plight of the Native American community. He would have gone to law school the previous year but … He broke off, and his face tightened. Elle did not press him. She was happy simply sitting there with Cree, whose serenity seemed to be gradually restored. Elle was discreet enough not to push him. Cree did say that he had his dreams. As a lawyer, he wanted to work for an environmental government agency but did not know how to go about it.

"Oh, I can help you with that!" Elle exclaimed. Then, without transition, she blurted out, "Do you have a girlfriend?" The words had come out without her realizing it, almost against her will. Cree looked at her, clearly puzzled, and a cloud reappeared on his face.

"Uh …" He gestured with one hand while continuing to drive with the other. He turned away from her and looked out the window. After a few minutes of awkward quietness, Cree turned to Elle again and, without answering her question, asked abruptly, "How about you? Do you have a boyfriend?"

It was Elle's turn to look away. "Ah, me." She drew a circle in the air with her hand. Then they both turned to each other and laughed. Elle thought that at that very moment, something had solidified the bond between them.

Soon they arrived at a wide spot in the river, lined with rice beds, where Cree had decided to put in the canoe. He pointed out the rice stalks, whose kernels were ripening in the sun. A blustery wind from the north bent the stalks and lent them a silvery shine. Cree aimed the canoe away from the shore and, holding out a helping hand, ushered Elle into the tippy craft. She felt rather giddy and narrowly missed going overboard.

"Hey, hey, easy, lady," he laughed, half catching her again as she stumbled. Did he see her change color? If so, he pretended not to notice.

This was Elle's second time in a canoe. She was still awkward with the paddle, but Cree patiently explained how to hold and stroke it through the water. Elle's athleticism came to her rescue, and they fell into a rhythmic paddling, interrupted at times by one of Elle's miscues. She giggled after having splashed Cree, who was remarkably good-humored about his partner's occasional blunders. He guided the craft with an expert hand. It was, Elle felt, as if he were one with the canoe.

They paddled against the strong wind that made dark blue swirls on the water. Little waves splashed up against the gunnels of the canoe. Paddling in tandem, the wind blowing through her hair and the sun shining on her face, Elle was on cloud nine. After a while, Cree decided to beach the canoe. He chose a spot in the shade of two large pines and tossed her a bottle of water that Elle thought tasted better than the most expensive Champagne at one of her professional receptions.

They were now talking in a carefree manner. Elle felt she was overcoming her awkward timidity, at least for right now, because words began to flow easily between them. Cree confided in greater detail his dreams of becoming an environmental lawyer and how, in addition, he wanted to help Native Americans protect their rights.

Elle, in turn, told him how being in this wilderness made her feel that she was beginning to live again. She learned so much from his talk about fauna and flora that never again would she look at the world in the same way. Beneath their trite words, they were really speaking to each other. They were saying, Elle was convinced, much more than either of them was willing to admit. After a good while, the conversation trailed off into a comfortable silence. Elle found a sudden interest in studying the pine needles. When she felt Cree's eyes on her, she looked up. Their eyes met for a moment before Elle averted her gaze.

After a brief silence that seemed like an eternity, Cree rose and said abruptly, "We should head back. It's getting late, and they'll be looking for you."

"My goodness, yes," Elle replied, feeling a bit relieved.

Once back in the truck, Elle fell asleep and did not wake until they reached the lodge. Cree stopped at the foot of the stairs leading to the office to drop Elle off. They looked at each other briefly. Cree leaned forward. Was there a hesitation on his part? Did he want to kiss her? Elle sat still. She held her breath. She both wanted him to kiss her and, at the same time, dreaded the gesture.

"Well ... good-bye," he finally said. Elle climbed out of the truck maladroitly. She tripped again and almost fell to the ground.

Something moved in the darkness. It was Amber. "Where have you been?" she demanded. "We thought you had an accident. I was worried." At first, Elle barely heard her daughter's words as she watched Cree wave. When the red taillights of his truck disappeared in the night behind the trees along the edge of the winding road, she tried to calm Amber down.

"Our guide just showed me the river and taught me how to paddle. It was great fun."

"I can only imagine."

"Did you have fun today with Lyle?" Elle asked.

"Yeah, but don't try to change the conversation. I'm not a virgin anyhow, so you don't have to worry," Amber threw out defiantly. The vehemence of her remarks was alarming.

Elle walked around the lodge on her way down to Whispering Pines to collect herself before heading back for another late dinner.

15

Daily Happenings—Wolves

THEY WOULD SPEND the next day canoeing the Loon River, which was frequented in the eighteenth century by the voyageurs to whom Tony referred as "those funny little men with large woolen caps." Singing, drinking, and paddling, these rugged souls traveled on waterways all the way from Montreal to Winnipeg and beyond, to points south, to exchange trinkets for beaver pelts.

Tony, Sherry, and Cree had joined the group that was finishing breakfast with the compulsory cup of coffee. Elle avidly studied every minute detail of Cree's face. When she turned her head, she saw Amber grimace in her direction. If Amber was aware of her mother's attraction to the young guide, did she see the young man as a threat ... or was she jealous of Elle? Was she, perhaps, interested in Cree herself? Amber gave her mother a lasting stare before turning back to Lyle, who seemed to be engaged in one of his unstoppable monologues about working for his campus newspaper.

Back at Whispering Pines, Elle was preparing herself for the outing when Amber suddenly irrupted into the cabin and let herself fall into the blue armchair. She draped her legs over the armrest, as was her wont, and stared into the distance. "So," she finally said. Elle didn't respond. "So?" Amber repeated after a moment with a meaningful intonation. "I want no shady dealings."

"Amber, I don't know what you're talking about," she said.

"You know what I mean." Amber's tone was gloomy.

"And what will *you* do today?" Elle asked in order to change the conversation.

"Hang out with boring Lyle," was the instant answer. Amber thrust her face into her hand and remained silent.

"All right." Elle rose, walked over to Amber, and tried to smooth her daughter's hair.

Amber bolted. "Don't," she said defiantly. "I'm not a baby." She rushed out of the cabin and banged the door shut behind her.

Elle was again shaken. Amber's passionate streak always erupted when least expected. Yet Elle's desire to go canoeing proved stronger than a concern for her daughter. After all, she had signed a contract with *Travel Magazine*. It was her job to explore the region. In reality, she had to admit to herself, she wanted to be with Cree.

After donning her jeans and T-shirt, she rushed to join the group at the parking lot but this time did not offer to ride with Cree. Mike noticed this detail and mumbled faintly, "Not today, huh?" Elle gave him a quick look and climbed into the van. Mike followed her. "Can I offer my shoulder again?" he asked, mimicking a chivalrous air. Elle had to smile.

They put in at the bottom of a rocky gorge. Tony told them to split into groups of two. "Hey, Elle, how about coming with me?" Mike shouted from afar. She could not decline his invitation. She looked toward Cree, and their eyes seemed to meet for a fraction of a second. Elle made the best of the situation and took the front seat in the canoe Mike was manning. A good sportsman, Mike had taken to canoeing quickly. He paddled in large, even strokes and guided the craft well, though, Elle mused, hardly with Cree's finesse. Cree was paired with Linda, who had eyes only for Mike and Elle. As for Elle, every time she looked in the direction of Cree's canoe, she felt as if someone had pinched a nerve in her.

With the sun at its zenith, Elle suddenly felt the heat. She tied a kerchief around her head and tried to adjust to Mike's vigorous strokes. Arriving at a first set of small rapids, Tony declared they should shoot them. Because of a lack of rain, the narrow passage turned out to be more like a minefield of boulders. They were using old aluminum canoes provided by the lodge that, judging from the scratches and dents, had experienced much hardship, and it was exhilarating feeling the thumps and the jolts when they hit the rocks. The canoes had a way of drifting sideways and getting stuck on top of invisible rocks. Old-fashioned chivalry came to the fore when the men offered to free the stranded canoes in which the ladies sat at the forefront. Mike twice rescued Elle, who laughed so hard she ached. He jumped into the stream and rocked the small craft when it seemed to get stubbornly stuck on top of a round boulder.

Cree was the only one who had steered clear of obstacles. He had already reached smoother waters at the bottom of the rapids and looked on calmly from a distance with his paddle resting across his knees. In the distance, Elle thought she detected a smile being aimed at her. Linda shouted some useless words of advice to Mike. After much laughter, noise, and splashing, they all reached deeper waters again and drifted downriver between high cliffs. They paddled by another oversized beaver lodge that Mike jokingly dubbed the Hilton. Cree informed them that the presence of fresh twigs on the structure meant that it was inhabited. Not a single aspen tree was standing in a radius of several hundred yards. Trunks were lying helter-skelter on the ground and in the water. The engineers of nature!

"The builders of civilization," Mike said added pensively, "but they sure make a mess."

They stopped to picnic on one of the large granite rocks that had been deposited by the Ice Age. Trying to steady herself to jump out of the canoe, she saw Cree, with laughter in his eyes, extending a helping hand. As he hoisted her on the rock, Elle shivered with pleasure. Sitting on the boulder, Elle gushed about the scenery as well as the fact that Marge, Betsy, and Ruth had prepared the most exquisite wilderness lunch ever.

Cree told them more about the river—about the importance of marshes that cleanse and absorb water, how rapids and waterfalls clean and oxygenate the river, and how the latter also helped wildlife, from fish to ducks and deer, from bears to wolves. He spoke of the precarious balance of the environment, which was subject to droughts, floods, natural plagues, and invasion by people. Elle felt that he was talking only to her.

During the rest of the trip, as they paddled downstream, she followed Mike's commands. Theirs was the second canoe. In front of her, she saw Cree and watched every one of his smooth movements.

On their way back to the lodge, they stopped at the International Wolf Center in Ely. Sitting in the amphitheater of the contemporary structure, they listened to a local guide's narrative about wolves and the difficulties they experience in today's world, including loss of habitat and disease but especially people's random and often unnecessary violence. At the end of the talk, the guide and her helpers went to call the wolves. Elle and her colleagues held a collective breath as several of the animals slowly and mysteriously descended from a small hill behind the center and calmly walked about on the other side of a glass partition.

Cree led Elle to an exhibit featuring the history of wolves. The animals' story from ancient times to this day resonated with her as she walked from station to station with the young man, listening to his words and the timber of his voice.

Upon Mike's recommendation, they finished the afternoon with a drink at a local outdoor restaurant on the main street. On a large deck decorated with flowerpots, the gang sat together on long shellacked benches made from tree trunks and ordered a couple of pitchers of beer and some pizzas. "With extra pepperoni!" Mike shouted. Elle ended up next to Cree. When they all had to move closer together to make room for Tony, she felt Cree's body against hers for the first time.

Cree did not stay for dinner at the lodge that night. To overcome her disappointment, Elle strolled down to the lake. The thought of Amber crossed her mind. Her daughter had made a point of coming to greet her mother and caught her again in the act of saying good-bye to the young guide, who was getting back into his truck. "Mother," Amber had admonished her sternly a few minutes later, "I want no fooling around." To Elle's questions about her own day, Amber had quipped that she had gone with Lyle to a park and gone skinny-dipping in broad daylight.

Elle dived into the lake, trying to push all thoughts of Amber out of her mind. Floating on her back, reliving the events of the day, she was overcome with a sudden surge of happiness. She stayed motionless and listened to the blood throbbing in her head. She felt that she was beginning to live again.

16

Ricing and Bears

Their last day excursion led them to a rice lake on a nearby Chippewa reservation. For decades, ricing had been a way of life for the resident tribe. Recently, with commercially grown rice and the community's revenue from casinos, harvesting the precious food had become less lucrative, yet it had not entirely lost its commercial or symbolic value. Now tourists were drawn to the activity as well. *Manomin*, or wild rice, was really wheat growing in shallow northern lakes or rivers north and south of the border. Cree had explained how people drive a canoe through the knee-high stalks. One person would stand or sit in the back of the craft while the other, seated toward the bow, would beat with a pair of wooden batons in alternating strokes on the upper stalks.

Elle delayed going up to the lodge so that she could ride with Cree, who seemed to expect her. She hoisted herself into the cab of the red truck and leaned back in "her" seat. This time, they took the lead. Cree talked about ricing, and from there the conversation drifted to the condition of the people on the reservation. He spoke with passion and, at times, even with indignation about the needs, hopes, and dilemmas of the Native American people. Elle was awed by Cree's animated features and regretted that when they reached the large, shallow lake covered with rice stalks, they were met by some natives who had volunteered to introduce the group to the art of ricing.

When everyone had arrived, Cree and Tony matched each person of the group with an experienced ricer. Elle could barely hide her disappointment when she was paired with an older tribesman, though Tony said he was the one with the most experience. Cree was to set out with Joan. Elle had no time to lament the fact that she was separated from him. Sitting in the bow of the slender craft but facing backward, she followed instructions from Joe, the old Native American, who patiently instructed her how to beat the kernels into the canoe by alternating the strokes. While Elle was beating on the stalks, Joe was standing in the rear of the craft, pushing and guiding it at the same time with a long stick. In the distance, the sight of Cree pushing his canoe through the stalks hit Elle to the quick. She dropped one of her batons.

"You're not concentrating," Joe admonished softly. "Beat on the stalk with regular rhythmic strokes."

Elle sighed and again gave herself over to what everyone referred to as the "craft of ricing." She beat on the reeds with her batons alternately with her right and her left arm. It was hard work, yet Elle began to find pleasure in gliding silently through the fragile stalks in the distant presence of Cree. When they gathered onshore after several hours, they agreed that ricing was the most rewarding activity. Carefully brushing the last kernels out of the bottom of the canoes, they filled several bags with the rice before driving off to a nearby place where the kernels would be processed, or "parched."

Cree led them to the house of Jim, an old Native American who was known in the area for his way of hand parching the rice. The operation took place in a specially constructed open shed that was kept in meticulous order. "Parching" was a high art. The kernels were poured into a large vat before being warmed and stirred over an open fire. At the end of this process, the old man explained, the kernels were ready to explode. He then poured them into a blower and ran them through on a conveyor belt several times, until the hulls had been discarded. They all got their turn at holding the big paddle and at moving the rice kernels around in the vat. The old man showed them how to move the kernels so they would not burn. Rod and Brett scurried about, taking pictures from every angle.

While the rice went through the machine, the group sat around in a circle on multicolored lawn chairs. Jim's wife, Denise, had plugged in a large coffeepot and brought out some local pastries. They indulged in the brew and sweets while exalting the mystical aspect of ricing. Sitting next to Cree, Elle maneuvered to delay their departure by expressing a sudden interest in an abundant consumption of Danish. "Elle, you have a real sweet tooth," Joan said with a tone of surprise.

They left with half a dozen bags of rice that had been neatly separated into categories according to the length and the quality of the grain.

Their last stop was at a nearby bear sanctuary that had been started after the death of an old loner who for many years had fed bears from his trailer. When he felt the time had come for him to go to a nursing home, he left his friends in the care of the newly minted American Bear Association. At the beginning, so Tony told the group, the bears were wandering around, mingling freely among the visitors. Now, a few years later, visits were more regulated. They took place at feeding time, at the end of the afternoon.

From the lot where they parked their van, they walked down to a platform to find a small crowd gathering and from where they could oversee a large area where bears roamed freely. Abundant literature on the platform covered every topic, from ursine nourishment to wildlife artists and holistic lifestyles. While devoted volunteers fed corn to the bears, a guide gave an explanation on the lives of the animals and their current difficulties in populated areas. Elle and Mike took copious notes. Brett and Rod dashed about, documenting all the action. Joan and Jim were having a hushed conversation with Cree. From the snatches Elle could hear, they disagreed with the very nature of the sanctuary, though they liked the idea of protecting a species paradoxically almost endangered in the wilds and abundant in the outreach of suburban areas.

The sun was setting bright red as they drove back to the lodge after a day filled to the brim with discoveries about the area and its people—for Elle, Cree's presence only intensified it.

17

Amber and Cree

Back at the lodge, the group dispersed. Cree stepped briefly inside the office to consult with Tom. As he prepared to leave, he happened upon Amber, who was hanging around the entrance door.

"Cree," she said in a low voice and gestured to him furtively.

"Amber, what's up?" Cree replied, smiling at her. For once, Amber seemed less hostile.

"Come, Cree, come over here. I want to show you something." Cree crossed the room. When he drew near, Amber said that she wanted to show him something in her cabin. "Please come now," she implored him.

"What is it?" Cree inquired with a puzzled look. "I do have to leave."

Amber had already turned around and was moving out the door. Cree hesitated. From the bottom of the stairs, Amber signaled again. "Cree, come on." Reluctantly, he finally followed the young woman down the path to Black Bear.

Once they were inside the cabin, Amber promptly closed the door behind them. She stood erect, facing Cree.

"What's the matter, Amber? What can I help you with?" the young man asked, taking in the room, with its disparate items of clothing and on the armchair what, judging from its title, looked like an open French book. "Is there something wrong?"

Amber hesitated. She shifted her weight from one foot to the other. "Nothing, Cree. Nothing is the matter."

"So can I go now?" Cree asked, this time in a joking tone. His words remained unanswered. "Where are Josh and Emily?" he asked to break the awkward silence.

Abruptly, without transition, Amber blurted out, "Cree, I love you. I really do."

Cree was unprepared for such an outburst. "But, Amber ..." he began hesitatingly.

"Yes, yes, I love you. Please, Cree. Tell me you love me too." Amber stood there motionless, her svelte body slightly trembling. "Cree, you're the one I want." She tore off her shirt and stood in front of the surprised guide. She was a beautiful young woman, and no one could be insensitive to her charms.

"Amber," Cree protested. "Amber, stop it."

Perhaps he succumbed to her momentarily or he simply wanted to be kind. He took a step forward and touched her bare shoulder. Amber threw herself into his arms.

"You do love me. I know you do. Please, Cree," she whispered tearfully.

"But, Amber, I can't do this. Besides, I am too old for you," he added after a moment. "And you're with Lyle." He grabbed her hands and disengaged himself gently. He bent down to pick up her shirt and handed it to her. "Put this on, Amber," he said firmly.

Suddenly, Amber's tears dried up. She held her shirt in one hand while standing in front of him with her bare torso. Her dark side came forward. "So I'm too young," she hissed. "But you're not too young for my mother!"

Cree became tense. "Amber, what are you implying?"

"You don't think I know? I've seen the two of you. You're all over each other." She put on her shirt without buttoning it and ran into her bedroom, slamming the door.

Through the closed door, Cree heard her throw herself on the bed, sobbing. He stood there dumbfounded and hesitating. He wanted to help her but then decided to return to his pickup.

Cree closed the door quietly behind him and looked around. He did not want anyone to see him, least of all Elle. He rushed up the steep path and went directly to the rear of the lodge, where the truck was parked. Tom came out of the office and seemed surprised at still seeing Cree at the lodge.

"I went down to the lake," Cree mumbled while getting into his the cab.

"Are you all right?" Tom inquired. "You look distraught."

"I'm fine. Nothing is the matter." Cree waved as he took off.

He was still troubled by his encounter, and as he was driving down the winding trail to the main road, he continued to wonder whether he should inform Elle. He finally decided against it.

18

Preparing for the Trip

A DAY OF rest had been planned before their long trip. The group lounged about the knotted pine table in the seminar room. Leaning against puffy pillows sewn with elk and bear motifs, they pondered their assignment while sipping large amounts of Loon Lodge brew from their green mugs. Mike proposed, and Elle readily agreed, that she should write the draft and he would edit it. Rod and Brett would insert their pictures. Joan and Jim would have a separate entry with data about geology, plants, and trees.

The DNR people did not show, and there was no sign of Cree. Elle had overheard him saying that he would be working on a project near Burnside Lake. During lunch, the sound of a car startled her. She raised her head and listened intently. Had Cree changed his mind? Did he want to see her, perhaps? It was a delivery van. Slinking back into her wooden chair, Elle barely masked her disappointment when she noticed her daughter's attentive gaze on her. Amber smiled and returned her attention to the mixed salad on her blue Fiestaware plate.

Elle withdrew to Whispering Pine for the afternoon. She thought about working and glanced at the computer that she had not touched since her arrival at Loon Lodge. She still could not get herself to boot it. After brewing herself a cup of coffee on the little electric machine that was part of the amenities, she sank deep into the blue armchair. Dreamily, she took a few sips from her mug and listened to the sounds from the woods and the lake, repeating Cree's words about the importance of embracing and loving the world. How different it felt after years of relying solely on data, spreadsheets, and worldly success!

Humming a tune, she finally rose to pack for the three-day wilderness trip. In addition to her T-shirts and jeans, she stuffed her gray hooded sweatshirt and a puffer vest into her backpack. In late August, the temperatures might drop down as low as the thirties, Cree had warned. Satisfied at last, she leaned her backpack against the chair near the door, from where she could easily grab it in the morning. Elle felt again the excitement of a little girl. She would spend three days in the company of Cree. They would paddle down rivers and lakes in the Boundary Waters. Together they would admire fauna and flora. They would visit rocks that Native Americans had painted several hundred years ago. They would camp together in wild, remote places!

After dinner, Elle lingered on the deck in one of the more isolated Adirondack chairs. Conforming to the daily rituals at the lodge, she had exchanged her cup of coffee for a glass of Merlot. Staring out over the lake through the pines, she imagined the days ahead.

"How is my beautiful Lady E tonight?" Mike's voice rang out. "Mind if I join you?"

Masking her annoyance, Elle gestured, and Mike pulled up a vacant chair. He fixed his eyes on her.

"Happy about the trip?" he asked. "You certainly look it. I myself am not thrilled about this camping stuff. At my age, I'd rather sleep in a good bed."

Elle smiled faintly. In front of Mike, she did not want to betray any sign of her secret excitement. She had spoken to the children after dinner and asked them to use extra caution and never to go anywhere alone during her absence. "Oh, Mom," Amber had retorted dryly. "It's not us you have to worry about—it's you."

"How come?" Elle asked with slight embarrassment.

"You mean you don't knooooow?" Amber said impishly, drawing out the word. She abruptly turned around and waltzed down the stairs from the deck, leaving Elle alone with her guilt.

Mike continued to speculate about the trials and tribulations of their upcoming journey. He seemed to harbor no hard feelings about his failed adventure with Elle. Was he simply good-natured or was he still hoping for a relationship? Darkness fell. A light breeze was blowing, and the crackle of crickets filled the evening air. In the sky above, the man in the moon greeted them. In another couple of days, the moon would be full. Mike pointed out Mars, Venus, the Big Dipper, and the North Star. Elle listened to his litany and followed his pointed finger absentmindedly. Suddenly, she wanted to be alone.

"Well, so long," she said, rising and pulling her sweatshirt tighter over her shoulders. "Tomorrow we'll have a long day."

"Yeah," retorted Mike, "and no mattress to sleep on. Better sleep tonight." Mike rose, grabbed Elle's hand, and gave her a kiss on the cheek. An awkward silence crept between them before they parted at the foot of the stairs and went in opposite directions. For a while, Elle saw Mike's flashlight dancing in the distance. Then all became dark.

She was already on the path following the luminous triangle of her own flashlight back to Whispering Pines when she heard someone call her name. Thinking it was Mike and silently cursing him, she turned around, surprised to see Tom's silhouette dimly lit by the bounces of his flashlight.

"Elle," he said when he caught up with her, "your mother's on the phone. She wants to talk to you before she goes to San Francisco."

Elle sighed. Her mother liked to call late, continuing to think the rates were cheaper. She accompanied Tom back up to the main phone in the office of the lodge and picked up the receiver. Trying to muster up some excitement, she said, "Hello, Mother."

"Elle! Hello, darling. I just wanted to call you before we leave for San Francisco to visit your sister, Ami. We're leaving the day after tomorrow. What should I pack? A dress from L.L. Bean's Traveler catalog? It's guaranteed wrinkle-free."

"Yes, Mother," Elle replied, "that sounds good."

"It tends to be cool there, so I'd better take a sweater too. I have a big wool sweater I bought at Saks the other day. I'll call you from Ami's to tell you how everything is going."

"Yes, Mother." From the booth, Elle looked around the empty dining hall and the table where, the day before, she had sat with Cree. Before she finally wished her good night, she distantly heard her mother say again that she would call her from San Francisco. Sighing, Elle hung up the phone.

Over the wire, her mother sounded even more mundane. And worse, she always had the knack of calling at the wrong time.

19

Elle and Amber

ANOTHER KNOCK ON the door woke Elle. It was Amber, who had come to tell her mother that the entire group except for her was already finishing breakfast. Amber sat down on her mother's bed. She pulled her left knee up and, while resting her chin on it, slowly looked around the cabin. Elle noticed that her daughter had been crying.

"Mom, be careful," Amber said. "I told you, I don't want any shady dealings. Got it?"

Elle smiled at her daughter's youthful admonishments. "Dearest," she replied, "there is nothing to worry about."

Amber threw her arms around her mother and started sobbing. "I love you, Mom. I don't want another man in your life."

Elle was alarmed at her daughter's new and passionate outburst. "And what about you?" she said with a smile, wiping away Amber's tears the way she had done so many times when her daughter was a little girl. "Will you go kayaking with Lyle? You watch out yourself."

Amber made a face from under her tears. "You have nothing to worry about. I know men only too well."

The declaration caught Elle by surprise. Still, she suspected that Amber, despite all her provocative talk, had not had many boyfriends and that Lyle might well turn out to be the first one.

"Well, I'll just stay with Josh and sweet Emily. They're safe. They already act like a married couple." Elle was struck by her daughter's astute description of her son and his girlfriend. For their young age and their playful and seductive manners, Josh and Emily did seem quite settled. Amber was more volatile.

Elle pulled herself together. "If you go somewhere, do tell the Ammans—promise? Always keep them informed of your whereabouts."

"Don't tell me what to do." Amber's dark side came forth again as she dried her tears. "I don't need anyone to tell me what to do. You just stay out of trouble yourself." With these words, she kissed her mother on the cheek and, again in the mode of a self-possessed young woman, turned abruptly on heels that squeaked, exiting haughtily.

What was her daughter trying to tell her? Had Amber noticed how taken she was with Cree? She rose and, still pondering the incident, put on jeans, a white T-shirt, and a long-sleeved flannel shirt. She looked at her backpack. Cree! Three days in the company of Cree! She felt a sudden rush. Her cheeks were flushed. Her daughter's menacing words quickly faded. She splashed a few drops of cold water on her face and brushed her teeth and her hair. With a pounding heart, she left the cabin to make her way up to the lodge.

PART IV

20

The Trip—Day One

BREAKFAST WAS STILL being served, and Elle decided to grab a quick bite. Most of her colleagues were already busy loading their backpacks into the van. Mike and Linda, indulging in a stack of pancakes, were the only ones left at her group's table. Mike was fiddling with his digital Nikon, which he jokingly focused on Elle.

"Hey, Elle," he greeted her, grinning, while Linda nodded coldly without an inkling of a smile. "Are you ready to learn the secrets of nature?" He laughed. "I'll write about the bears that feast on us innocent campers."

"Oh, Mike," Linda guffawed feebly.

Elle smiled and poured herself some Loon Lodge brew. At a neighboring table, the Ammans were devouring hash browns with eggs and Canadian bacon. Lyle was sitting away from them, plainly pining after Amber.

"Okay, Elle," Otto Amman said while chewing on a large piece of bacon, "we'll keep an eye on the kids." He laughed.

Amber shrugged her shoulders and muttered, "I wonder who needs supervision around here."

Josh and Emily arrived through the sliding doors and greeted everyone. Josh waved with his usual charm. "So, Mom, you're off on your big adventure? Bon voyage! Not to worry—we'll be good. Won't we?" He looked at Emily, who was beaming, probably at the prospect of having Josh all to herself. The young woman continued to smile radiantly in Josh's direction. These two were lost in their own world.

"Thanks, Otto," Elle responded. "I'm sure the youngsters will be okay. I'm glad to know they can turn to you and May for help." She felt Amber's foot kicking her shin under the table. "Thanks so much," Elle reiterated, slyly looking at her daughter.

"Oh, you are very welcome," Otto replied in all seriousness. "We thought we'd take them into Ely. We'll have lunch on Main Street and shop for gear. Isn't that what they call it?" Otto laughed at his own wit.

Tony arrived to announce that the new Wenonah canoes, light crafts good for traveling long distances, had been loaded onto the trailer. They were ready to head out. Elle kissed her children good-bye, and after some last-minute motherly advice that was met with laughter from Josh and another defiant stare from Amber, she followed the others, heading through the office and out the back door.

The sun felt hot on this late summer day. The hum of the van's engine seemed louder than usual. The side doors of the van were wide open. Except for Mike and Elle, everyone was already seated inside. Cree's truck was parked to the side. He was standing next to it, the way he had been on the first day Elle met him. He appeared to look at her, smiling. Elle slowed her pace. Mike suddenly proposed to ride with Cree, but luckily for Elle, Linda protested loudly. She did not want to let go of her man. Mike made a gesture as if he wanted to say something but followed the wishes of his partner. By the luck of the draw, Elle now had no choice but to ride with Cree. This maneuver did not escape Amber, who happened upon the scene with Lyle in tow. She simply stared in the direction of the red pickup.

"Be good." Elle tried a smile while gesturing toward her daughter.

"Look who's talking!" Amber repeated.

Elle felt herself blush as she climbed into the cab of Cree's truck and settled into the passenger seat. Doors slammed, people shouted good-bye, engines revved, and they were off, leaving waving people behind them.

They drove down the familiar winding road amid the tall pines and up to the intersection with the county road. Cree pointed out the old white across the road. He never failed to comment on the magnificent tree, whose branches spread far and wide over its massive reddish-gray trunk. Cree loved that tree, saying that it could tell many stories.

Elle also admired it each time anew, but especially when she rediscovered it through Cree's eyes. Cree made the turn onto the county road with ease. He followed the van, driving in silence. For Elle, it was bliss, full of unspoken longings and, she mused, perhaps of understanding. Any pangs of guilt on her side had vanished.

She leaned back and took in the landscape as they drove along the shady trail along which tall aspen, birch, and pines alternated between low marshes and beaver ponds. Along either side of the road, large patches of bright yellow petals of black-eyed Susans shined amid the last daisies of the season. Grouse scurried off the path. The smell of the North Woods permeated the air that wafted through the open windows. Elle turned and looked at Cree. She was convinced that she would never tire of admiring his fine features. She lingered again on his thin but sensuous lips before checking herself. He was so young. As if he had felt her gaze, he turned toward her and smiled. It was, Elle thought, a happy smile. She felt elated about riding at this moment with Cree in the warm morning sun. They continued their journey without talking.

"Excited about the trip?" Cree finally uttered.

"Yes, of course," Elle answered. She looked straight ahead. Through the cloud of dust in front of them, she saw the outline of the van.

"You know, since we talked, I did get an application for the law school exams," he confided. "Thanks to your help. You've been great."

Elle melted.

When they arrived at their launching place, they found that the other members of the group had already unloaded and packed the canoes. Soon they pushed off. Tony and Sherry were the leaders, while Jim and Joan followed them. Next came Rod and Brett, then Mike and Linda. Elle and Cree were the closers. The original plan had been for each member of the DNR to pair with a member of the group. Since Rod wanted to paddle with Brett and Linda could not let go of her Mike, the two leaders were put in one canoe, with Cree and Elle in another.

They paddled between low banks lined with reeds. The ash trees along the water were just beginning to turn yellow. Beyond them, aspens and birches stood out against the blue sky, while towering over them, the branches of the white pines reached out into space. They glided over the translucent waters of the shallow river. Slightly ahead of them, the other canoes alternately disappeared behind the tall reeds, only to reappear at another bend.

Cree was steering. Sitting in the bow, Elle heard the even strokes of his paddle. She turned around. Cree had removed his shirt and now wore his red bandana around his forehead. His ponytail was untied, and his hair was playing freely around his shoulders. The outline of his sinewy body stood out against the sun. His muscles were moving under his skin. His long fingers clutched the paddle with a gentle grip. Each time she looked at him, something touched Elle to the quick. Cree's presence affected her in a way that no other man's had in many years. At times, she was convinced that Cree felt the same way; then again, her hopes faded. He was so young, she kept repeating to herself. Cree simply looked at her, with his quiet, enigmatic air.

She turned back, facing forward again. Ducks fluttered in front of the canoe, kicking up water. A blue heron, standing upright like a wooden stick, decided not to give up his fishing spot. She heard Mike and Linda alternately laughing and squabbling in the distance. Over the thick reeds, she spotted the heads of Tony and Sherry, who were moving along at a steady pace, still followed by Jim and Joan. Rod and Brett appeared to be zigzagging while taking pictures, trailing in the others' wake.

Cree made the canoe move along effortlessly. If he was lagging behind the others, it must have been on purpose. At least, Elle liked to think so. She was so alive. Without even seeing Cree, she felt his presence all about her. Closing her eyes, she listened to the occasional cry of a raven and to the guttural sound of an occasional eagle that Cree had taught her to recognize. As the warm sun caressed her body, she abandoned herself to the rhythm of the paddling, changing from one side to the other.

In a wider part of the river, they finally reached a rocky outcropping where large pine trees offered shade. Tony and Sherry signaled that they should stop there. They beached their canoes on a narrow sand bar and jumped out, hungry as wolves, as Mike put it, after their hard paddle, which was one of pure delight for Elle.

*   *   *

The current picked up in the afternoon as the five canoes were moving swiftly through the luminous waters. No longer paddling in any fixed order, they alternately passed each other or paddled side by side. They followed the river that had carved its way through the now hilly and then rocky countryside over thousands of years. A distant and continuously thunderous noise announced a set of rapids downstream.

"You wanna portage?" Tony and Sherry shouted.

"We'll shoot them!" Cree yelled back. "Right, Elle?"

Startled, Elle turned to meet Cree's laughing, slightly mocking eyes. Now she had to prove herself. "Of course!" she yelled back defiantly.

Cree could barely mask his surprise. "All right, Elle, hold on. We're off."

They passed Linda and Mike who were arguing about what course of action to take. Linda was trying hard to talk Mike into portaging. Elle quickly turned around just in time to see their craft shoot by a sign bearing the icon of an upside-down broken canoe, announcing danger ahead. She had a moment of remorse and wished she had opted for the safer route by land. But there was no turning back. The powerful current had already carried off their canoe. Little waves started to lap at the gunwales.

"You tell me where the rocks are!" Cree shouted from the back over the deafening noise of whitewater.

"But I can't see them!" Elle protested.

"You have to guess!"

She strained her eyes as they were dashing down the rapids, carried by the waves. Cree navigated deftly around the boulders. "Oh, there's a boulder!" called Elle. She dropped her paddle and grasped the side of the canoe. Cree quickly shifted the direction of their craft. The boulder scraped and rocked the canoe and water gushed, in but they were safe.

"Oh," said Elle, "I'm so sorry." Her courage had left her. Cree laughed. He clearly had shot rapids thousands of times before.

After they reached calmer waters, Elle sighed, happy at having been made fun of and proud for having participated in this new adventure. Tony and Sherry came down at a safe distance behind them. Resting in a quiet pool, they joked about Elle's first real whitewater experience while waiting for the other members of the group to arrive. Everyone except for the guides had opted for the portage.

Jim and Joan were first. "Our West Coast fitness conditioning paid off," Jim said with a grin. In turn, Rod and Brett appeared, looking their cool and unruffled selves. Mike came staggering out of the woods after a long time, juggling the yellow canoe on his back. Huffing and puffing, Linda followed, the canoe pack on her back and the paddles in her arms. They obviously had been arguing again.

"Linda should have let me join you guys!" Mike called. "These new *ultralight* canoes weigh a ton!"

The river widened into a large wilderness lake dotted with islands and bordered by rolling ridges. "We'll camp on the main shore of this lake. I know of a good campsite in a grove of pine trees at the foot of a hill," Tony assured everyone.

While they were paddling across the lake, Elle pointed to a pair of loons swimming in the distance. One opened its wings and let out a haunting cry that seemed fitting to the milieu. "A warning cry," Cree told her. "The birds feel intruded upon by our group and signal danger."

When, their bodies aching, they finally reached the campsite, they marveled at the pristine spot whose tall red pines and birch groves stretched all the way down to the lake. On the flat part near the beach, Tony and Sherry chose a tent pad near a fire grate, where some leftover logs were neatly piled. The area would serve as their main camp. Tony and Sherry unloaded the food from their massive Duluth pack, furbished for this kind of venture. They hoisted it high up onto one of the large branches of a pine to keep their victuals out of the reach of the bears. They were going to pitch their tent nearby. Linda insisted that she and Mike should stay there as well, for whatever real or imaginary safety reasons. Rod and Brett decided on a more remote place on a small hill from where, as they put it, they could enjoy the sunset. Jim and Joan located their preferred spot farther in the back.

Elle explored the terrain in yet another direction. She found a little opening a couple of hundred feet away, near the far end of the sandy beach. She unfolded her pup tent. She could barely hide her thrill when she noticed that Cree had laid claim to a spot just beyond hers. A complete novice, Elle deciphered her book of instructions while trying to assemble the pieces of her tent. The structure collapsed several times, once even with her inside. Laughing at Elle's desperate maneuvers, Cree approached and expertly helped her assemble the structure. Elle looked up at Cree, who stood near her with the same unperturbed, radiant smile. Did Cree feel the way she did? She suddenly wondered anew with a fresh pang of anguish if he felt anything. If so, he was good at masking it.

Cree went to put up his own tent while Elle arranged the inside of hers and took special care to spread out her oversized sleeping bag. She looked at it dreamily for a brief moment before pulling her oversized hooded sweatshirt tighter around her shoulders. There was a sudden chill in the air, as the sun was beginning to set. In late August, the days were getting shorter.

She made her way back to the main camp. Tony and Sherry, with the help of Jim, Joan, and Mike, were busy finding more kindling and logs for the fire. Linda was worrying about blisters on her hands after a long day of canoeing. She grimaced while putting on some healing lotion.

They would grill the fish that Tony had caught that afternoon and fry potatoes in the hot oil of the same pan. Sitting near the fire on a large log in the company of her new colleagues and Cree, Elle listened to the crackling fire as she watched the day fade into the night.

21

The Night

After dinner, Mike passed around a plastic flask filled with bourbon. When they got little tipsy, conversation flowed freely. Mike recalled climbing Machu Picchu in Peru with a friend. On the summit, sitting on top of a high cliff, they had shared a bottle of wine, and because of the thin air and the altitude, they became quite inebriated. They were unable to climb down and had to sleep off their hangovers. Everyone laughed at the story, especially at the way Mike told it, in his ever-droll and self-deprecating way.

Silence eventually fell over the group. The only sound was that of burning logs. By now, it was quite dark and, at least for Elle, a bit eerie. They heard rustling and a faint thumping noise in the bushes.

"A bear," whispered Mike, forever the joker.

Linda gave him a mean look. "Not funny," she chided after a few seconds.

Tony stoked the fire, throwing a couple more branches on the smoldering logs. The flames shot up high into the sky and illuminated the lower branches of the pines. Sparks flew through the dark night. The fire was romantic, but somehow it also had something menacing to it.

"Oh, look!" Brett sounded alarmed. He pointed toward the east, where, above the jagged tree line, a dark red shape had appeared. At first, it looked like a bloody, monstrous creature. Tony and Sherry laughed.

"It's the moon," Linda exclaimed innocently.

It was indeed the moon rising behind the trees. It was almost full and rose rapidly into the sky, where it quickly became smaller and paler. Its bright light projected a long shaft on the calm waters. A beaver swimming across the lake left a silvery V-shaped trace behind. Helped by the nocturnal setting and the bourbon, the conversation gradually became more intimate, and they began to talk about their lives. The darkness of night and the tight circle they formed around the fire brought them closer together.

Elle listened to Mike, who rehashed his divorce, and then to Joan and James, who talked about their years together and the resistance of James's spouse to his proposed divorce. She never liked these confessional stories and was afraid it would be her turn soon. Not wanting to be put on the spot, she decided to take leave. Even though Cree was still there, she rose and, under the pretense of fatigue, bid every one good night. Without turning on her flashlight on the moonlit night, she courageously followed the narrow path along the water to her own tent. Instead of retiring, she sat down at the foot of a pine tree to admire the clear late summer night.

In the distance, the voices and the intermittent laughter of the group cut into the night. She thought about her marriage. In retrospect, she thought, it was Max who was always buried in his documents. At least, that's how she now saw it. She was beginning to feel that the marriage had been stifling. She had lived according to sanctioned codes. Sure, they had all this worldly glory and beautiful things, but had she really been living? She and Max had pursued professional success, but while doing so, had they lost their souls and the world? Is that how Max had felt too?

She heard a rustle behind her. She jumped and barely refrained from screaming. Then she realized that it was Cree. He had left the campfire and was coming down the path between the pines. Was he simply going to his tent or was he following her? She held her breath and remained immobile. Cree came straight toward her and sat down. They remained silent for a couple of minutes.

"Do you like this?" he asked in his hushed voice, without specifying. The trite question seemed electrically charged.

Elle turned her head toward him and smiled. "It's beautiful." Then she looked straight ahead at the water again. She was physically aware of Cree's being there. She turned back toward Cree, who was still looking at her. Their hands moved closer on the pine needles that covered the sandy ground. Their fingers clutched. Cree leaned forward. His lips found hers. He pushed her gently back onto the ground. Elle could feel his hands moving over her body while she, in turn, clutched the thin and muscular body that she had coveted so much.

"Sweet," he murmured. "Sweet ..." His words echoed in her ears. From a distance, she heard the group's voices and laughter before she became oblivious to the world.

They lay there well into the night under the vast expanse of the starry sky. Elle felt the cool breeze caressing her body. She was now leaning against Cree's shoulder. Max had never been able to stay awake. After making love, he always drifted off into sleep and began snoring. Cree stroked her gently and pulled her toward him. They lay together for a while longer. When Elle rose and quietly walked the short distance to her tent, Cree followed her into the tent. They made love again, passionately groping for each other in the moonlit night.

Elle fell into a deep sleep. When she awoke, all was perfectly still. *Everyone must be asleep*, she thought. The eerie hoot of an owl briefly troubled the stillness of the night. Lying by her side, Cree was breathing quietly and regularly. She touched him lightly and went out into the dark. The moon had set. Above the heavy mist that was shrouding the lake, the nocturnal sky scintillated with myriad stars. She sat motionless and breathed in the cool air.

At last, she reentered the tent. Cree stirred and put his arm around her. It had been over two years since Max had left, and the presence of another body troubled her. She felt the gentle touch of Cree's hand on her hip before she drifted back into sleep.

When she awoke again, it was broad daylight. Cree had left. She heard voices and the clinking of pans. The faint smell of a fire wafted through the tent. It must be breakfast time, Elle conjectured, stretching and yawning. She remembered the events of the night and smiled happily. Deeply moved by last night's encounter, she felt an unexpected shyness while walking over the small hill toward the fire.

Mike looked up to greet her. "Hey, Elle. Are you our sleeping beauty again?" Linda darted a glance in his direction.

Elle turned crimson as Cree, who was stoking the fire, paused and looked up at her with squinting eyes. She could see a smile on his face and what she guessed was an almost mocking expression in his eyes. He looked at her laughingly but remained silent. Elle was a touch unnerved as she sat down on a log.

Sherry passed around a plate with pancakes. Still laughing silently, Cree sat down next to Elle and handed her a cup of coffee. His hand touched hers, and their eyes met. Elle shivered with pleasure.

"Look up!" cried Mike. They turned their heads slightly toward Mike. He pushed down the button of his camera. "Got you. Excellent," he said after scrutinizing the replay. "Souvenir from the wilderness!"

Much too soon for Elle, Tony rose and announced that they should strike camp. Today they would canoe to another nearby lake and would pause to look at painted rocks. The scenery would be rugged, cliffs on the edge of the lakes and rapids cutting through the fault lines of the landscape. They had several lengthy portages ahead. They all voiced regret at having to leave this idyllic campsite. Most of all, Elle was reluctant to disassemble the tent where she had known such intense happiness for the first time in many years. They put out the fire and loaded the canoes. Elle turned around and looked one last time at the place that had become so special for her.

22

Day Two

RIDING IN THE canoe with her lover, Elle felt giddy all day. She and Cree did not talk much as they paddled downstream in the swift, translucent waters. They were, she thought, in harmony with the world and clearly in love with each other.

They paddled between steep rocky embankments. They portaged over several small but steep hills along the edge of precipices. Finally, after traveling along low, rocky stretches of the river, they arrived at another lake, this one larger than the first. Tony told the group that he knew of a lunch spot that was well worth the wait. Reluctantly and with aching muscles, they agreed to persevere, with the exception of Elle. Being in a canoe with Cree gave her a new level of energy. Their paddling, she felt, was a way of making love.

Judging by the number of scratch marks from canoes on the exposed bedrock, the promised island must have been a canoeist's favorite. They unloaded their lunch packs and decided on a swim—except for Sherry, who promised to set up their lunch, and Linda, who was still afraid of lakes where real fish dwelled.

Elle swam out in the deep water. From the depths, something suddenly grabbed her. She let out a scream before she recognized Cree, and then she giggled with sheer pleasure. She began to splash her lover; he caught her by the waist. Together they played a dunking game with the carelessness of children. In a flash, she recalled the image of Josh and Emily back at the lodge. She remembered her own glum condition. Now she was living again. The scene clearly did not escape Mike, who, when they returned to shore, remarked that when some people go into nature, they begin to regress into childhood. Instead of blushing, Elle burst into a healthy guttural laugh.

The long dark blue lake was bordered by a thick forest and low yellow reeds connected by way of narrows with the Boundary Lakes proper. Over centuries, Cree and Tony told them, flowing water had carved out a narrow passage through the high granite rocks that, as part of the Canadian shield from the Precambrian period over a billion years ago, spanned from the Arctic Islands to Minnesota, from the West to the coast of Labrador. These rocks were the site of the Indian paintings that Cree pointed out to the group.

They paused and held the canoes in place in front of the buff- and gray-colored rocks to behold what looked like reddish graffiti. The shutters of Rod's and Brett's cameras began clicking again. Joan and Jim launched into a flurry of questions. Elle scribbled every detail in her pad for future reference. She joked with Mike that she was taking notes for two. Sioux or Chippewa, Cree told them, painted the pictures long ago, possibly while standing in canoes. Their meaning was not clear. Cree elaborated, saying that the human figure with large extended hands, the moose, and what looked like a wolf could mean something totally different from what they seemed to represent. They sat in awe, wondering about the sublime mysteries of bygone cultures.

The narrows opened onto Lake La Croix, a long and narrow body of water with hundreds of islands. It would be easy to get lost without a guide. Cree took the lead. He seemed to know all the narrows and every island. By late afternoon, they had found a designated campsite on another rocky outcropping. Elle again chose a spot away from the group, and Cree opted for one behind hers. Mike remarked how tents were far apart yet so close together in this deserted spot. Elle felt herself blushing. Cree just offered one of his unreadable smiles. To hide her embarrassment, Elle chose to go for another swim.

The water and the evening breeze felt soothing. Several miles away, a plume of smoke from another campsite rose straight into the air. The sun was setting, and the jagged outline of the trees grew darker. She felt light, cleansed of bad memories. The past and the divorce had abruptly receded into the distance. Gone was a feeling of solitude, even her anxiety about the future. She was living fully in the sensuous surroundings and the company of her new lover. She could not tell if she had discovered the world through Cree or Cree through the world, but she knew that something had touched her and was transforming her. She had left far behind what now seemed like an empty world of cocktails, receptions, and endless self-promotion.

Back on shore, she put some extra care into arranging her face and hair. She finally felt ready and walked over to the fire to join the others. By now, Mike had taken out a second plastic flask. He looked at it wistfully. Well, the wilderness has its drawbacks. Gentleman that he was, he started passing the flask around without helping himself first. They all felt mellow after a long day of paddling and with several sips of Knob Creek in their veins.

The fire was burning bright, and while waiting for the flames to die down so they could put the fish Tony had caught on the iron grille, they sat idly about on logs and rocks. Elle passed Mike's flask on to Cree, who looked straight into her eyes with the peculiar penetrating yet slightly mocking glance of his and grinned. His teeth were flashing. His gaze flooded Elle with a powerful feeling of joy. She smiled back happily.

It was almost completely dark when they heard a deep howl. "Wolves," Cree and Tony said almost in unison.

"They are getting ready to hunt," Cree added.

"Remember, they don't attack humans," Tony added, after seeing that the faces of group had turned a shade paler even with the glow of the fire.

The howl was eerie, and the group was far from reassured by Tony's words. They listened intently for the howl to repeat itself, but they were only met by the vast silence of night.

The conversation lagged. They all felt tired after a full day of paddling and decided to retire. Elle had not exchanged a word with Cree, and she wondered if he would follow her again. She sat down at the foot of a pine tree outside her tent. No one came. She stayed there for a long time, motionless and with a growing sense of disappointment.

She was already rolled up in her sleeping bag when she felt Cree's presence in the tent. He had come in so quietly that she had not even heard him open the front of the tent.

"I've inherited this from my ancestors," he murmured with a chuckle in response to her remark. He slipped under the covers with her. They looked for each other in the night and found each other again.

❧ 23 ❧

Day Three

T HEY WERE RELISHING the pancakes cooked over the open fire, garnished with some of the last wild raspberries, when Tony announced that they should move on. They were to paddle to a place where two Cessna floatplanes would pick them up. The planes would drop them off at a resort on one of the Border Lakes nearer their lodge. Elle grew tense again. She realized that her time with Cree would soon end. She turned to look at him. Did he read her thoughts? Was there a trace of sadness in his smile?

Elle felt that the rhythm of their paddling in the morning was slightly off. Neither of them spoke. When they made a short pause at one of the many small islands, she managed to sit next to Cree at some distance from the group. Elle was first to talk.

"This is our last day together."

Cree nodded. "I know."

"Cree, I cannot bear the thought of not seeing you again." Elle held back her tears. The sky had quickly lost its brilliance. The heat was bearing down on her. "Cree, why don't you come with me and go to law school at Lincoln University?"

Cree shook his head and looked straight ahead. "That's impossible."

"Why?" Elle insisted. "Nothing is impossible. We've got to make it possible."

"No, Elle, I cannot. I don't want to be separated either, but I belong to this place and you belong to the city—and you know it." He rose abruptly and walked over to talk with Tony.

Elle was distraught. What was the matter with him? When they resumed their journey, she felt edgy. They paddled until they reached the pier of a lodge, where two bright yellow floatplanes with red stripes were waiting for them.

As they unloaded their canoes at the pier, Mike praised to the sky the fact that he would soon be able to sleep in a real bed again. Elle was so heavyhearted that she could not even muster a fake smile, much less utter a word. She barely touched the fried walleye that the owners of the lodge had carefully prepared and that was being served to them on rough-cut wooden tables behind tall windows facing the lake in a spacious beam structure. She distractedly listened to Rod and Brett conferring about their photos.

Cree seemed to have suddenly distanced himself. Why was he acting so strange? Was he sick of her? Had he simply taken advantage of her? Had she misread him? Had she been duped? Now that he had gotten what he wanted, was he just ready to move on? He was no better than Max. Would he pick up another naive female on his next guided tour? Elle nursed her coffee and silently cursed Cree.

Relief came when Tony announced that the planes were ready for boarding. "Do they strap the canoes on the planes? How many people do these planes seat?" she distantly heard Mike ask the pilots. After Elle entered one of the planes, her eyes veiled by tears, she found herself next to Cree. Had he put himself there deliberately? He took her hand, but

Elle disengaged herself and turned toward the window. Cree did not try again but only looked straight ahead.

Moments later, the pilot revved the engine and took off. The plane began to hover over the watery surface before slowly rising into the clear late summer sky. Elle distractedly looked at the landscape below. She registered the chain of Border Lakes and the seemingly endless forests without being able to appreciate their splendor. It was a quiet trip back. Joan and James, who were seated in the same plane, must have been thinking about their impending separation as well. Tony, the fifth passenger, commented abundantly on the places over which they were flying, from the Boundary Waters to Quetico Provincial Park in Canada. He got little response to his enthusiastic travel commentaries. Noticing the sullen faces around him, he soon fell silent himself.

When they touched down, the other floatplane had already arrived. Mike greeted them from the dock. "Let's go have a beer on the deck of the lodge over there." He pointed toward a distant wooden structure. "Hurray, we are back in civilization. I will sleep in a real bed tonight," he kept repeating. "Hey, Elle, Joan, Jim, Cree, let's drink to this."

"Yeah, let's do it," Tony, Sherry, Linda, and even Rod and Brett chimed in. In contrast to Joan, James, Elle, and Cree, they seemed to be a cheerful bunch.

They all walked over to the nearby lodge with a large deck that overlooked the rocky Border Lake. Mike and Tony assembled a couple of the parasoled tables. Elle was morose. The smell of fried food made her nauseous. A bright-eyed blonde server brought out bottles of Bud Light and cheese fingers that Mike had ordered.

"Ha! Some hearty fare after this wilderness delight," he said.

Inwardly, Elle cringed. Outwardly, she did her best to put on a good face. She raised her glass in unison with the others and toasted to the success of their project.

"A special cheer to our guides!" cried Mike. They all toasted again to Tony, Sherry, and Cree.

Elle thought that Cree's smile was fake. He seemed tense. His lips were tight, and she thought she could see that dangerous little flame in his eyes again. He finally grabbed her hand under the table and whispered in her ear, "Let's go out in the back for a minute. Walk through the restaurant and exit through the rear door. You go first. I'll follow."

Elle was happy to leave the table. After letting a few minutes go by, she pretended to go to the restroom. She crossed the dark lodge redolent with a stale smell of fried food, only to exit through the back screen door. Outside, in the blinding sunshine, she paused and leaned against the wall of the lodge. Her heart pounded when she heard footsteps. Cree rounded the corner of the lodge.

"Let's go," he said. He grabbed Elle's hand and pulled her in the direction of a wooded area with hiking trails in the back of the lodge. They walked briskly up a steep hill. Cree led Elle away from the main trail, into the woods. When they were some distance from the path, he paused near a large aspen.

Elle leaned against the tree trunk. "Cree, I want to be with you," she said, tears choking her voice. "Come with me."

Cree leaned over her with his hands against the trunk. "Look, Elle, I don't want to be separated either," he managed to say.

"Then come with me." Tears began streaming down Elle's cheeks. "You can study law at Lincoln U."

Cree's face tightened again. "That's impossible," he repeated, turning from her.

Elle sobbed louder. "You just took advantage of me. Do you do this with all the women of the wilderness parties you guide?"

Cree seemed strained; he covered her mouth with his hand. "Elle, don't. Don't say these things. We have given each other so much. Let's not spoil it." They looked at each other.

"Cree, I love you."

"I know you do. I love you too, Elle." Cree leaned over Elle and started kissing her slowly. Soon they fell to the ground and began to make love on the forest floor. Cree pulled Elle's shirt off, and his lips started to move down her body.

*　　*　　*

When Elle opened her eyes, she looked up at the crowns of the aspen trees lit by the setting sun. Her tears dried up. She managed a smile. Lying next to her, Cree propped himself up on his elbow and stroked her hair.

"Cree, I want to see you again. Come to the farewell party tomorrow. We will be together one last time. You can stay with me."

"Elle, I can't," he declared. "I have plans that cannot be changed." He looked decisive. "Besides, what would your daughter say?" he added in a less abrupt, more conciliatory tone, vainly trying to introduce a logical argument. Elle started sobbing again uncontrollably as she dressed.

Cree blurted out, "All right, I will come. I will meet you in your cabin at ten p.m. Leave the party early. I don't want to come to the party or see the people. Let's go now." He seemed irritated suddenly. "The others will be looking for us." He rose abruptly and started to head back, then he stopped, turned around, and waited for Elle, who felt triumphant.

When she caught up with him, Cree put his arms around her and began kissing her as if, she felt, for the last time. They finally let go of each other. Elle felt ashamed at having behaved so lowly.

"Oh, Cree," she said from under her tears, "you've given me back my life. I don't want us to part. When I'm with you, I feel so alive." She looked at him and gestured vaguely in the direction of their surroundings. "You've helped me see the world in a different way."

"We've both changed," Cree replied, "but, Elle, the change is going to outlast our time together in this place. We both look at the world with different eyes. Let's go. The others will be looking for us."

The large van with a new driver that would bring them all back to Loon Lodge was parked outside the main building. He would drop off the group at the lodge and continue with Tony and Cree to the jump-off point, where they could retrieve their vehicles. The canoes and backpacks had been loaded. Everyone was already aboard, looking for Elle and Cree. Mike spotted them.

"Hey, youngsters. Where have you been, my romantic Lady E?" He looked at her and added covertly, just so she could hear it, "Lucky fellow."

Elle ignored the insinuation. She climbed in the van and sat down in the last row, behind Rod and Brett. Cree stayed in the front with Tony. The motion of the van made everyone drowsy. Elle was still sobbing quietly, though Cree's words were slowly sinking in. Cree was right. The change she felt would outlast her presence in the North Woods, but could she live on without Cree?

It was already dark when they reached the lodge. They climbed down from the van and retrieved their bags. Tony, Sherry, and Cree would continue their journey.

"See you tomorrow!"

"Thanks, guys!"

Everyone was shouting happily, except Elle, who still had a heavy heart in spite of Cree's persuasive words and the fact that he had promised to come see her one more time.

Tom and Jenny came out of the lodge to greet them. "Hey, everyone," said Tom. "We kept you some supper. You're late."

"It's because of Lady E and our guide. They got lost in the woods." Everyone laughed, and Elle could feel herself turn crimson.

Amber had appeared on the scene. Elle hoped that her daughter had not overheard Mike's joke.

"Mom, how have you been?" Elle was surprised at hearing her daughter's tone. "We're inside playing games."

"Guys, why don't you come inside and eat?" Jenny interrupted. "You can go back to your cabins afterward."

"Good idea!" Mike shouted. "Ah, Jenny's cuisine … Will taste twice as good after all the wilderness stuff."

Elle could not muster an appetite. She could still taste the cookout of the previous night. She could feel the breeze and hear the little waves lapping on the shoreline. Above all, she could hear Cree's hushed words and feel the touch of his hands on her body.

24

The Farewell Party

THEY CONVENED ONE last time in the seminar room of Loon Lodge to discuss the logistics of the piece they were to submit in a few days to *Travel Magazine*. Rod and Brett displayed their digital photography, which drew high praise and laughter. There were candid shots of Mike struggling to hold up the canoe, of Elle emerging from the waters, and of Sherry and Tony wrestling to get their craft off a rock. Joan and Jim announced that they would focus on geological data but also on the impact of development and the challenges of climate change for the area.

Mike was resolute again that Elle finish the draft on people, fauna, and flora and then send it to him for a quick read. She was more "attuned" to the surroundings and had more "firsthand experience," as he put it with a wink of the eye. Pretending not to notice the intimation, Elle nodded politely with as much of a professional air and composure as she could muster. Throughout their session, she had a hard time hiding her impatience. All she could was think of was Cree. She wanted the day to go by quickly so that the magic hour would arrive.

Elle was happy when she was able to excuse herself after lunch. She stopped at Black Bear, but the children had left. They must have gone on a last outing. She returned to her cabin and opened the windows to breathe in the oxygenated North Woods air. She sank into in her armchair and looked around. How changed she felt. It was only a week since she had left the city and she was a different person. She felt so alive and so aware of the world around her. Her heart was still heavy at the thought of having to leave Cree, though, for now she could only think of his impending visit. She would somehow try to convince him to come with her. Could he adapt to the city? There were lakes and parks ... and they could come back here for summers. Cree had opened a completely different world for her, and in so doing, he had enabled her to reconnect with herself. Yet somehow, she still wanted him present. Elle was confused. She checked her watch. It was two o'clock. A long wait was ahead.

Instead of packing, she decided to prepare for Cree's visit. What if Amber came? Oh well, she'd have to invent an excuse. She rose to move the sofa closer to the fireplace and align the coffee table. Stepping back, she looked at the arrangement before fetching a tray with a bottle of wine and two glasses for the coffee table. She would have to pick a few flowers from the woods. Finally, Elle went into the bedroom, smoothed the coverlet, and repositioned the pillows. She hummed a tune to overcome a slightly nervous feeling.

After what seemed like a long time, she checked her watch again. Six more hours! Time was crawling. To make it pass, she could go for a last swim or read over her notes before dutifully attending the farewell dinner and party with her colleagues and the other guests. The Ammans, the Daniels, and the Groziers were also leaving the following day.

Lyle was walking around with his head hung low. Amber showed little pity for him—or else she was good at masking her game.

Elle wandered down to the lake for a last swim. The wind had died down, and the air felt unusually hot and humid for the season. Large storm clouds were towering in the distance. She thought she heard the distant rumbling of thunder. She dived into the cool waters.

Refreshed, she readied herself for the evening. As they had decided to go casual, she stepped into her camp uniform one more time. She chose a tight camisole and a shirt she could take off—just in case. She remembered Mike telling her that she was acting like a teenager. Okay, so then ... She made a dismissive gesture, smoothed back her hair, and set out for the last dinner at the lodge.

The tables were set for the festive occasion. Everyone was already assembled with the exception of Cree. Jenny, Marge, Betsy and Ruth had outdone themselves with a five-course gourmet dinner consisting of local specialties from another fish fry, which sweet Emily abhorred, to a last blueberry pie. White and purple asters adorned the tables, now in white porcelain vases. Mike opened a couple of bottles of wine. Marge, Betsy, and Ruth lit the candles. Everyone was exalting the North Woods hospitality and vowed to return to Loon Lodge at the first occasion.

"Hey, how about an anniversary dinner a year from now?" Mike suggested.

They raised their glasses in unison again and thanked their hosts and their guides.

"Where is Cree?" Joan suddenly asked.

"Couldn't come," Tony answered. "He was busy at home."

"Too bad. Nice-looking guy," Rod added dreamily.

Mike glanced at Elle but refrained from commenting. They soon turned their attention back to Jenny's last blueberry pie.

Later they moved the tables to prepare for dancing. Jennie, Marge, Bessie, and Ruth brought out more food and drink for the evening. The women's boyfriends arrived, followed by Tony, his wife, and Sherry with her partner. Even John Makala and his spouse, Mary, drove up for the occasion. Only Cree was missing.

"Odd fellow," Mike now ventured, scrutinizing Elle, who remained impassive. "Wonder why he couldn't come," he added, then focusing his attention on the bar.

Feeling the effects of the wine, everyone was soon in a jolly mood. Josh, sweet Emily, Amber, and Lyle had set up shop in a corner. Elle caught Amber's scrutinizing stare. Had she guessed something? Did Elle look nervous? She tried to lend herself to the joyous atmosphere. She accepted a dance with Mike and even let him hold her close. She bounced up and down with Tony. They all did a polka dance and exchanged partners up and down the line.

Outside, the wind rustled the leaves and bent the branches. Through the open doors and windows, they now saw flashes of lightning. "Good thing we're safely back here and not on a campground," said Linda. Her observation was met with general approval, except from Elle, who still wished it were otherwise.

The storm moved closer. In spite of the loud music, the noise of thunder prevailed. "You have to count between each flash of lightning and the thunderclap that follows; each second represents a mile," said Joan. "One, two … five, six. Six miles away."

The next flash of lightning lit the trees and was followed by an even louder thunderclap. Elle checked her watch. Twenty more minutes. Time just did not seem to move. Mike invited her again and spun her around. She felt dizzy. At the end of the dance, she decided to make her exit. Lyle had just pulled Amber toward the back of the lodge and the moment seemed propitious.

"Okay, guys," she said, "I'm going before the storm hits. I have a long drive ahead tomorrow. I'm tired. It was great to work with you and to get to know you. We will all be in touch about our piece. I look forward to a reunion next year."

Staving off protests, she dutifully made the rounds, kissing and hugging those with whom she'd spent the last week. She left through the sliding doors just as the first drops of rain began to fall.

25

Waiting for Cree

S TILL WAVING, ELLE disappeared into the dark night. At the foot of
the stairs, she listened for the sound of Cree's truck but heard only
the faint howl of the wind. With the help of her flashlight, she strode
quickly down the familiar path to her cabin. Cree should be coming
any minute. She wanted to tidy up the cabin before his arrival. A flash
of lightning illuminated the path. She counted to three before a loud
thunderclap followed. The storm was now only three miles from the
lodge. The rain started to pour by the time she entered Whispering
Pines for one last night with her lover. Elle looked around the space
that, like the outdoors, had been transformed by her encounter with
Cree, even though he had never actually set foot in the cabin. Her eyes
moved over the hand-hewn log desk and the chair where her city gadgets
were sitting idle.

She no longer deplored the fact that she was in one of the few
pockets in the entire country with no cell phone connection. Soon
she would be back in the city with all its noise and glitter. She would
be deafened and blinded. But even there, she was beginning to sense
that her life would be different. The brief stay in the North Woods had

helped her overcome the gaping emptiness of her existence that was revealed to her after Max's departure. Through her encounter with Cree, she had rediscovered the world in all its beauty and fragility.

Sitting while waiting for Cree, she flashed back to Rawling Moulter III's reception a few weeks ago, when, from the vantage point of another blue chair, she had scanned a living room filled with mundane glory that, at the time, heightened her own sense of solitude. Now, with a new feeling of connectedness, she looked over the small living room of the cabin. She decided to light the logs in the stone fireplace. The storm made it damp enough to warrant a fire not only for its warmth but also to contribute to the romantic atmosphere. She smiled as she looked at the crossed snowshoes above the mantel.

Having lit the candle in the decorative hurricane lamp on the table and with a good blaze in the fireplace, she sat down again and almost timidly glanced toward the log bed under its green, brown, and beige quilted cover. How she longed for Cree. Closing her eyes, she felt Cree's delicate hands on her body. She heard the peculiar hushed sound of his voice and saw the shine of his inquisitive dark laughing eyes. She relived the last two nights in rapid succession: their embrace, the silence, the chill of the early morning, the lone cry of a loon, and the mist shrouding the calm waters at dawn.

She looked up at the paneled window framed by the white gauze curtains. It was completely dark outside. The aspens were rustling in the stormy night while sheets of rain were gliding over the roof. A lightning bolt illuminated the woods and part of the lake. Almost instantly, the rumble of thunder shook the little cabin in its foundations and made her jump. The eye of the storm was now at the lodge. A gust of wind suddenly blew open one of the windowpanes.

Elle looked at her watch. It was a few minutes past ten. Cree should arrive any minute. He was always punctual. Like a nervous bride, she rose one more time to rearrange the brightly colored wildflowers, and that's when she heard a knock. With her heart beating wildly, Elle rushed across the living room and unhooked the lever of the door. She was ready to throw herself into Cree's arms but stopped dead when she recognized Tom under his dark green poncho, which was dripping with rain. A storm lantern was swinging from his hand. He grinned at her.

"Elle, I'm glad you're not in bed yet." He looked around the room. His eyes paused on two wineglasses set out on the table. "Having a party?" He laughed good-heartedly.

"Oh, no, it was from before," Elle mumbled, somewhat distraught.

Tom changed the subject. "Elle, you have a phone call. It's your mother again. I didn't want to disturb you, but she says it's urgent. She wanted me to come and get you."

Elle's heart sank. She felt like cursing her mother. Her mother had said she would call from San Francisco, but why did she have to choose this very moment? Elle sighed but put on a smile. "I'll be right there."

"You'll need some rain gear," Tom said. By now, he was looking at the flowers. "You like elegant living, don't you?" he said, looking at her with a meaningful glance.

Elle just wanted him out of the cabin. She grabbed her yellow rain poncho and a flashlight. The absence of cell phone service, which only five minutes ago she'd counted as a blessing, had now become a curse. What would Cree think if he arrived and she was not there? She closed the latch behind her without locking it, hoping that Cree would at least try the door.

Tom suggested that they take the upper fork of the path that led directly to the entrance of the lodge and the small room with the telephone. "This way," he said with a smile, "you don't have to say good-bye to all the folks twice."

The short walk up to the lodge seemed like an eternity. She entered the phone booth and picked up the receiver. "Hello, Mother," she said, faking a cheery tone.

She heard her mother's nasal voice. "Elle … at last. It must be terrible to be up in the wilderness without even a cell phone connection."

"Oh, no, Mother, quite the contrary. It's been wonderful."

"Never mind," her mother answered. "I must tell you, San Francisco is just extraordinary—and your sister is doing so well."

Elle listened distractedly and glanced through the glass panel at the part of the living room that was visible to her. She saw Josh and sweet Emily dancing close to a slow tune. Lyle had returned and stood in a somewhat gawky and expectant position near the sliding doors. He seemed to be staring out into the dark, stormy night. She could not locate Amber. Perhaps her daughter was in the area of the living room hidden from view, Elle speculated while listening patiently to her mother's detailed narrative.

"Well, I must tell you, Elle," her mother resumed, "yesterday Ami gave us a tour of the vineyards in the Sonoma Valley. It was very hot, but my new dress was perfect for the occasion. Really wrinkle-free."

Elle felt that her patience was being tried. "Yes, Mother, how interesting," she answered politely.

Elle was burning. She wanted to get her mother off the phone to go back to Whispering Pines so as not to miss Cree. Her mother hung on with unusual stubbornness.

26

Amber's Betrayal

L YLE HAD BEEN successful in luring Amber to the seminar room in the back of the lodge. They lingered for a while on the cushioned benches. Lyle fidgeted and rubbed against the bear and elk motifs on the padding. "I can't believe we're going home tomorrow," he finally managed to say, his voice trembling with emotion. Amber remained shrouded in silence. Lyle drew Amber near and began kissing her. She was unresponsive but let it happen. For a while she consented but then brusquely tore herself loose and signaled that they should go back to the party.

Amber looked around for her mother. "Hey, Josh, where's Mom?"

"She left," Josh replied laconically.

"Why did she leave?"

"I don't know," Josh retorted, shrugging his shoulders. "I guess she was tired. She mentioned the stress of the drive ahead. What's wrong with that?"

Amber was suspicious and wanted to follow her mother, but Lyle pressed her for another dance. They were again playing a slow tune, and Lyle yearned to hold his reluctant partner tight in the dimmed light.

Amber submitted to a few pirouettes with the lanky young man whom she both liked for liking her and despised for being so awkward.

After the first two numbers, she disengaged herself abruptly. She threw her head back. "I forgot something in my cabin," she blurted out. Rejecting Lyle's gallant offer to brave the rain and go fetch the mysterious missing object, Amber ran out the sliding door into the dark, wet night about the very time her mother and Tom Silver entered the lodge through the main entrance.

Hurrying past her cabin where the light was still burning, Amber ran straight to her mother's cabin. She knocked but got no answer. Finding the door unlocked, she let herself in, half expecting to find her mother with Cree. There was no one inside. She noted the tray with two glasses, the candle flickering in the hurricane lamp. Her heart pounded. She sensed her mother's presence. Holding her breath, she glanced into the bedroom. Everything looked as if her mother had prepared for a special occasion and not for her departure.

Amber tiptoed around, came back into the main room, and let herself fall into the blue armchair. She stared at the glasses on the small wooden table. The rain was now hammering on the roof. Lightning bolts zigzagged through the sky beyond the trees, followed by deafening thunder. Suddenly, there was a discreet knock. Amber rushed to the door. She collected herself and took a deep breath before opening. In the frame of the door, in the pouring rain, outlined by the light streaming from inside the cabin and by lightening from the outside, there was Cree.

They stood face-to-face, and Cree finally attempted a smile. "Why, Amber," he finally managed to say, clearly trying to stay calm.

"Why, Cree, does this surprise you?"

"Well, no, not at all."

The two sentences were followed by another awkward silence. A minute passed that seemed like an eternity.

"What are you doing here?" Cree asked. Then, almost in a run-on sentence, he asked in his hushed voice, "Where's your mother?"

Amber retreated into the cabin, and Cree crossed the threshold. Amber was now triumphantly sitting on the edge of the desk, dangling one leg provocatively in front of Cree. This was the hour of her revenge. The tables were turned. She feigned innocence. She had a completely disinterested look on her face as she stared straight at Cree and with a half smile asserted, "My mother isn't here." After a slight pause, she added, "My mother sent me here. She asked me to tell you that she didn't want to see you."

Cree turned visibly pale. His lips turned into a thin line; his chin became more angular. His eyes contracted, and Amber could see a dangerous flicker in them that she had not seen there before. She still sat on the desk but felt less sure of herself. She was immediately frightened.

Cree stared at her for a few seconds. He seemed not to see her. Clearly trying to compose himself, he replied, "Tell her I stopped by to see her." After a moment, he added, "Tell her good-bye for me." With these words, he turned sharply, went swiftly out the door, and vanished in the dark.

Amber stood immobile. She felt like running after him, but something held her back. She stood in the doorframe and silently shouted Cree's name. Through the pouring rain, she stared in vain into the stormy night.

Cree was gone.

27

Mother and Daughter

Amber stepped back into the cabin and dropped into the easy chair, feeling both shaken and triumphant. Now she was even with Cree, who had so rudely rejected her. But had she done the right thing? A few minutes later, she heard footsteps. Was Cree coming back?

* * *

Elle noticed the door ajar and the soft glowing light streaming from the cabin. Expecting her lover, she entered swiftly and with a smile. No less surprised than Cree to find Amber in her cabin, Elle stopped near the door.

"Amber, why aren't you up there dancing with Lyle? What are you doing here?"

"Nothing, really … nothing," Amber replied slyly. "Surprised to see me? I just stopped by to see how you were."

"Well," said Elle, looking around, "I'm fine. I just talked to your grandma, who says hello. She wonders how you are. She'd like to see you."

"We're supposed to visit her for Thanksgiving, remember?" Amber answered.

Before closing the door to keep the rain out, Elle took a long look outside, just as she had been looking around the cabin when she first entered. She listened intently, thinking she heard a noise. "Did you hear a car?" she muttered, half as a question and half as if to reassure herself.

"You seem nervous," Amber said. "Are you expecting someone?"

Elle tried a smile. "Oh, no, it's just the thought of leaving and of having to take care of many things beforehand." She made a vague gesture.

"So why did you leave the party early? Don't you like the people?" Amber persisted.

"Oh, no, that's not it. I'm just a bit tired from the long canoe trip. I wanted to collect my thoughts and write down some of my impressions of the trip while they're still fresh. Besides, we have a long drive ahead of us."

"Yeah, sure," Amber quipped rather sarcastically. "Who are the wineglasses for, anyway?"

"No one. They're just for decoration."

Amber became more menacing. "Yeah, sure, some decoration."

Elle was again listening intently. "Did you hear a car door?"

"No," her daughter replied, "it was probably just a falling branch."

"Aren't you going back to the party?" Elle asked.

"Why, do you want me out of here?"

"Oh, no, not at all. I'd love you to stay, but Lyle might be waiting for you." Elle knew she was a bad liar. She could hear the fake tone of her own voice.

"You know I don't care about Lyle."

The storm began to calm, though it was still raining hard and thunder rumbled in the distance. Elle and Amber continued their standoff, Elle becoming more anxious with each passing minute. She was also feeling a growing sense of disappointment.

By now, Elle had sat down on the sofa. She looked at the glasses and beyond them, through the open door and into the bedroom. Where was Cree? Why was he so late? What might have kept him?

Amber watched every one of her mother's moves shrewdly. Their forced conversation had come to a halt.

28

The Accident

S UDDENLY, THE SOUND of a car did beckon. Cree? Elle and Amber
rose in unison and listened in silence. Noises were coming from
the lodge. People were shouting. Grabbing a flashlight and her yellow
rain slicker, which she held over her head, Elle bolted out the door,
her heart pounding. Amber followed her mother up the steep path,
stumbling over pine roots and rocks.

When Elle turned the corner of the lodge, lights flooded the area
and showed people running about. Through the open door, Elle saw an
unknown man on the same telephone where she had been talking to her
mother only a short while ago. Tom sat in the passenger seat of an idling
truck. The door on the driver's side was open. The stranger on the telephone
slammed down the receiver and, pulling on the visor of his baseball cap,
came running out the door, climbed into the truck, and drove off with Tom.

"Could someone tell me what's happening?" Elle shouted with an
ominous feeling as she saw Tony getting into his car with Sherry and
her boyfriend.

Mike had started running down the road. He heard Elle's question
and, without stopping, cried out to her. "There's been a bad accident

on the county road, right at the entrance of the Loon Lodge road! Two local guys came upon it and one just drove up here to call the police."

By now, everyone seemed to be running down the winding trail to the intersection at the county road. Elle joined them. She was frantic. She ran in the dark night without noticing the rain that was hitting her face. *Cree!* The thought flashed through her mind. Did Cree crash into another car when he turned onto the lodge trail?

From a distance, through the trees, Elle faintly saw the scene that looked as if it were illuminated by powerful lights. A vehicle was engulfed in flames. People were standing around, looking on helplessly. Elle stopped at the scene and remained stock-still. "Can't somebody help? Can't someone do something!" she shouted.

Mike put his arm around her shoulders and muttered, "Elle, there's nothing to be done."

Elle stared at the wreck of the car that had smashed into the great white pine. The impact was so great that the car had burst into flames. Whoever was inside could clearly not be helped. She guessed more than she saw the outline of a truck. The rear having been somewhat preserved, the license plate was still partially legible. She knew even before deciphering the number: it was Cree's. Elle felt faint. A car came racing down the county road. It was the sheriff.

"Boy, a good one," he said, getting out and looking at the wreck. "No one could have come out of this inferno alive."

By now, Mike and Tom had recognized the license plate as well, and the comments from everyone began.

"Cree! How is this possible?"

"What was he doing here? Did he decide to come to the party?"

"But it looks as if he was on his way out. Why didn't he come in?"

"He collided head-on with the pine tree. Was he trying to avoid a deer?"

"There aren't any skid marks. Odd. Did he lose control over his vehicle?"

"Cree was such a good driver."

"But the night was dark and rainy. Visibility was poor."

"Cree knew the road well. He traveled it many times. The driver of this truck made no attempt to turn at the end of the side road. Was it an accident?"

"Or," Elle heard someone murmur, "a suicide?"

Amber, who had arrived on Elle's heels, grabbed her mother's arm as if she were drowning. Elle felt her daughter's trembling body leaning against her own. The proud teenager was reduced to silent tears. Elle suddenly knew. Cree had come. He had come while she was on the telephone with her mother, and he had found Amber in the cabin. Her daughter must have said something that made him leave. What did she say? Did she tell him that Elle didn't want to see him? That also explained why she had heard the engine of a car while she was speaking with Amber. Why had she not run out? Elle glanced at Amber. Her daughter was pale as a sheet and staring straight ahead at the burning vehicle. Amber was no longer into playing games. She was now in shock.

Elle distantly heard the voices of people who continued to speculate about the cause of the accident.

"Was Cree going to fast"?

"Had he not seen the end of the road"?

Elle stared at the tire marks that went straight to the old pine tree that Cree loved so much. Dead man's tree! Josh's innocent joke crossed her mind.

Cree, why, why? Elle shouted internally. Was it really an accident? Did a sudden flash of anger make him drive too fast? A suicide? Impossible! He had so much to live for.

The flames were beginning to die down as the rain picked up again. The outline of the truck became more visible. Elle shuddered when she saw the charred remains of the cab in which she had sat with Cree and in which their passion had begun. Mike looked at Elle intensely. She knew he understood.

They all stood around the burning truck just as they had done around the campfire only a couple of days earlier. Everyone looked exhausted.

An ambulance came speeding down the road. There would not be much for the drivers to take. A volunteer fire truck also arrived. A few men jumped out and began to spray foam onto the flames. The fire was soon reduced to mere smoldering from which small flames still shot up here and there. Slowly people began to turn around and walk back, trying to explain Cree's presence and the fact that he was driving out when he had not come to the party.

"Odd man," Rod said.

"Charming and handsome … but so intense," Brett said.

"A real shame. So young and so promising," Joan added.

The sheriff and the volunteer firemen stayed at the scene to wait for the tow truck.

Elle was still riveted to the spot. Tom came over and encouraged Elle and her daughter to go back to the lodge. He assured her that nothing more could be done.

A lone car passed, stuffed with people probably returning late from a local bar. They stopped to look. "Boy, I guess this one had a few glasses too many!" Elle shut her eyes. Cree was not a heavy drinker.

Mike broke away from Linda and, ignoring her glare, hugged Elle. He too urged her to go back to the lodge. "Amber needs you," he whispered. He handed her his jacket. "Here, this is for your daughter."

Tom urged the remaining guests to walk back to the lodge. The storm had abated. Thunder continued to roll in the distance, but by now the rain had almost stopped. Elle put the jacket over her daughter's shoulders. She turned her around and led her back up the road.

When they arrived at the lodge, Josh and Emily greeted them. "Hey, where was everybody? When we came back from Black Bear, we were left alone. Did you all go skinny-dipping in the rain," joked Josh.

Elle managed to reply in a faint voice. "There was an accident near the large pine tree down the road. It was Cree. H-he's … dead."

Josh's mouth fell open. "Oh, man. At the dead man's tree! Amazing." He told his mother how sorry he was and then turned to Emily. "I guess the party's over. Let's go back to Black Bear." He took her by the hand.

Elle took Amber back to Whispering Pines. She put her wet and shaking daughter in the bed she had prepared for Cree and herself. She covered her daughter, who was still sobbing, with blankets and stroked her hair, urging her softly to get some rest.

Back in the sitting room, she opened the window and collapsed into the blue armchair, where she sat immobile for a long time, staring at the platter next to the two glasses on the table in front of her. She poured herself a glass of wine and emptied it in one gulp. She looked up at the half-open window. It was completely dark. The rain had stopped. She could hear the tapping sound of raindrops falling from the roof of the cabin onto the wooden deck. The temperature had dropped, and a cool breeze came in through the window. Elle stared blankly into the night.

PART V

29

Death and Renewal

ELLE AWOKE FROM a heavy sleep when someone began pulling on her arm. It was Amber, who pronounced her usual words: "Mom, it's late."

Elle noticed that her daughter had swollen red eyes and looked pale under her summer tan.

"I'm going to my cabin to see if Josh and Emily are there."

Elle nodded. The memories of the previous night returned, and the pain resumed. Elle felt drowsy and shaken. Her limbs ached from having slept in the armchair.

"I'm going to have breakfast at the lodge," she told her daughter. "Will you join me?"

Amber acquiesced silently as she was leaving.

Sunshine poured into the cabin. The sky was clear, and the wind had shifted. It was coming from the north; Elle could tell from the occasional clouds that were racing through the sky. The leaves of birch trees along the water now stood out bright yellow, interspersed with the brilliant red of a few maple trees. The storm had cleared many trees of leaves too. The landscape looked more autumnal, and the water shone through the trees a deeper blue.

Still in a stupor, Elle looked at the splendor while she relived the tragedy of the previous night. Cree was dead. Gone. Never again would she hear his voice, see the brilliance of his laughing eyes, or feel his touch. Yet even through her pain, she somehow knew that returning to the city would be different. Cree's words echoed in her: *To forget, you have to go outside of yourself and reconnect with the world* ... But by what cruel twist of fate did Cree have to die? She silently called to him. *Cree! Cree!*

Slowly Elle dressed. When she put on the shirt she wore on the trip, she thought she could detect Cree's faint smell.

She wandered up to the lodge for breakfast and met up with her daughter. Everyone was dazed and subdued. Elle asked Tom if she could stay another two days or so to attend the funeral. In response, the burly man gave her a gentle hug with tears in his eyes.

The Ammans, who were preparing to leave, offered to take Amber, Josh, and Emily. There was room in their minivan, and they could drop the kids off en route to Cincinnati. Lyle looked expectantly at Amber, but she asked to stay with her mother. Elle was rather surprised but happy about her daughter's decision.

Over breakfast, they slowly began to exchange Cree stories. They talked about the softness of his manners and his physical strength. They remembered how gentle he was, though not without an occasional flare of anger.

"Such a shame." Mike shook his head pensively as he was pouring more coffee. "Such a talented young life."

Elle listened in silence. Amber sat hunched over her plate without touching her food. Elle thought she saw tears glistening on her daughter's cheek.

The Ammans left after breakfast, with Josh and Emily smiling and waving from the back of the van. Lyle had kissed Amber, but she'd remained stiff.

After embraces and promises to stay in touch, the rest of the group soon departed. Mike gave Elle one last hug that was now more one of comfort than of seduction.

Elle returned to Whispering Pines, where she packed a few remaining items before sitting down at her desk for the first time since her arrival in the North Woods. She would try using the day to begin a draft of her piece for the magazine.

She looked out the window at the vivid color of the early autumn sky, the landscape that stood in all its splendor, indifferent to the tragedy that had happened the night before. Through the trees, Elle saw a lone kayak slowly moving across the lake. *Amber?* she wondered. Through the half-open window, she breathed in the smell of the earth, made stronger by the rain. She listened while smiling inwardly to the true "whisper" of the pines, punctuated by the calls of a few feisty blue jays.

Suddenly, a desire welled up inside her. She sat down at the table and opened her computer. She closed her eyes, paused, and then quickly began to write:

> *There is a place up north, along the Canadian border. It is full of blue lakes, silvery streams, and lush forests. Fauna and flora abound. The land is both vigorous and delicate. It beckons you to look at it, to listen to it, and to tread lightly upon it ...*

Elle wrote all day and well into the night. She briefly paused for a light dinner with Amber, who still looked pale but composed, before returning to her desk. The writing flowed as she remembered Cree's words and the sound of his voice. She recalled the sights and smells of the North Woods and Cree's touch while they were sitting on the beach or lying in the tent. It was as if he were dictating for her. She wrote of the necessity of believing in the world while respecting its beauty and its fragility. At times, she heard Cree's indignation over so much neglect and incomprehension. She wrote with passion and conviction of the boreal forest and its clear waters, frolicking deer, stealthy bears, and elusive wolves. She wrote of the splendor of the place and the challenge needed to sustain it.

*   *   *

The day of the funeral, Tom and Jenny gave Elle and Amber a ride into town. The local church was filled to the last seat. Elle and Amber had to stand in the back. Native rites were to take place later. The terrible and mysterious accident had attracted the entire town. Everyone knew and liked Cree, though not all agreed with his ideas.

The priest spoke kindly about the brilliant young life that was so tragically taken from his family. He remembered Cree's love of the area and his dreams. The music swelled as tears flowed freely.

After the service, the entire assembly went to Forest Cemetery. Elle silently called out to Cree, whose presence she felt stronger than ever. The family lined up near the simple pine casket that was about to be lowered into the freshly dug grave. Elle could hear sobbing around her. She did not dare turn her head. She identified Cree's father and stepmother, who stood motionless near the casket with one of their own daughters.

Next to the latter was another young woman with long dark hair, carrying a baby in her arms. "That's Mara, Cree's girlfriend. They were planning to get married this winter," she heard someone explain in a whisper in answer to a hushed question.

So that was Cree's secret. That was why he would not come with her and why he always had to go home. Tears welled up in Elle. She felt saddened, yet at the same time, she felt almost joyous. "Cree," she whispered. "Cree lives on."

She stood motionless. Amber's head was now leaning against Elle's shoulder. Amber was shaking and sobbing uncontrollably while huddling against her mother. Elle put her arm around her daughter.

❦ 30 ❦

Driving Home

MOTHER AND DAUGHTER drove back to the city in silence. "You know, Mom," Amber said unexpectedly, removing the earbuds of her iPod, "I finished that French book." She did not comment further. Elle simply nodded.

The trip, she mused, had turned out different from what she had hoped. It had renewed her bond with Amber unexpectedly. The encounter with Cree and his tragic death seemed to have changed them both and brought them closer together. More and more, Elle felt that her encounter with Cree was more than with a single person. It was, as Cree himself had wanted it, with a place but even more so with a way of being in the world. That place could be anywhere, in the North Woods or in the city. Cree was so wise for his young age. He was at once calm and passionate. At times, he became enflamed. It was perhaps one of these moments that had led to the accident. Cree wanted to be a lawyer who cared about the world, not someone who strove only after vain success, the way she and Max had done for so long.

After they arrived home, Elle overheard Amber talking on the phone to one of her friends. "I feel so grown up now," her daughter confided to an invisible interlocutor.

Elle was soon sitting at her desk, shuffling through papers, an activity that marked the beginning of a new academic year. Elle looked at a picture of Amber on her desk. How her daughter had changed over the summer. Amber looked taller, thinner, and her features more determined. She had become a young woman bearing a trace of sorrow on her face. She would fly off to college on the West Coast the coming weekend. Elle could not accompany her but had promised to visit soon. She had to return to her own university.

31

Another Reception

RAWLING MOULTER III had another reception, this time for new faculty. For the occasion, he had assembled his trusted team of faculty and administrators, Elle counting among them. She had once again made the rounds and was now, a month later, sitting in the same blue wing chair in the living room of the presidential mansion. As she scanned the room, she thought of a blue chair in the North Woods.

Familiar faces were standing around amid a few new ones. Waiters glided around, this time balancing trays with red and white wine instead of the Champagne and heavy hors d'oeuvres. From a group near the French doors that were now closed, Kirk Haywood emerged with his usual broad smile. He came over to greet Elle.

"Hey, Elle. Have a good summer? How were those woods? No bear got you? You look different; you radiate something. I read the draft of your article for *Travel Magazine* that you sent me," he added, continuing to look at her inquisitively. "A page-turner, really, written with uncharacteristic sensuality. Quite a surprise, coming from you ... Ready to go out now?"

Elle smiled back at him and shook her head. "Not quite yet. Mourning takes time, you know."

"Too bad it's taking an awfully long time. Whenever you're ready. I'm here." He pirouetted on his heels and walked back to his group. He turned around one more time and silently mouthed the same words: "Remember, I will always be here."

Elle smiled again, knowing she was ready to leave. She walked over to the president and shook his hand.

"My dear Elle, must you leave already?" Rawling Moulter III's words were identical to those he had pronounced just weeks earlier.

She mumbled something about needing to get back, and five minutes later, she found herself on the same road, driving down between the two rows of mansions that now exhibited autumnal colors with their yellow, rust, and dark red mums. This time, while driving back to her apartment, she mulled over her stay in the North Woods.

After waving to the doorman, she collected her mail. On the tenth floor, she entered her apartment decisively. The children were both gone. Josh was back in New Hampshire, and Amber was now at Berkeley. Elle was alone. Yet she no longer dreaded her solitude.

She sifted through her mail. There was a small letter package with no return address. She recognized Mike's handwriting. She went into her study, sat down, and opened it. On a blank note card, she read "souvenir of the wilderness," written in Mike's hand. She unwrapped the tissue paper. It contained a framed photograph of her and Cree.

It was a picture of them sitting on a log at their campsite on the morning after their first night together. As he had handed her a cup of coffee, their hands touched slightly. They'd both looked at each other and smiled happily, as she remembered, when Mike snapped it. Through the slender tree trunks, one could see the glistening platinum-colored waters of the lake from which mist was still rising.

Closing her eyes for a moment, she relived the scene: the sunlit lake, the light breeze, the faint smell of the fire, and the chatter of voices against the early morning stillness. She looked at the picture for a long time.

She heard Kirk's comments: "You look different; you radiate something." Elle looked up from the photograph.

Elle looked beyond her reflection in the window, over the tops of the trees in the park on the other side of the street and out over the lake. She went to open the window. The cool autumn breeze flowed into the room. She heard the waves crash onto the beach. Elle smiled sadly but with a bit of joy.

She booted her computer and checked her e-mail. She opened a message from her sister, Ami:

> *Elle, how have you been? I had a good visit with Mother. How was your trip to the North Woods?*

Elle pushed the reply key and began to write:

> *Dear Ami,*
>
> *I met a man up north. His name was Cree. He profoundly changed my life. He helped me reconnect with myself and with the world ...*

CPSIA information can be obtained
at www.ICGtesting.com
Printed in the USA
FFOW04n0217270815
16354FF